W9-BOK-082

· HARCOURT BRACE & COMPANY ·
1919–
1994
· SEVENTY-FIVE YEARS ·

Sweet Friday Island

THEODORE TAYLOR

HARCOURT BRACE & COMPANY

San Diego   New York   London

Sweet Friday Island

Requests for permission to make copies of any
part of the work should be mailed to:
Permissions Department,
Harcourt Brace & Company, 6277 Sea Harbor Drive,
Orlando, Florida 32887–6777.

Library of Congress Cataloging-in-Publication Data
Taylor, Theodore, 1921–
Sweet Friday Island/Theodore Taylor.
p. cm.
Summary: Vacationing on what they think is an uninhabited island,
fifteen-year-old Peg and her father find their adventure turned into
a fight for survival.
ISBN 0-15-200009-7
ISBN 0-15-200012-7 (pbk)
[1. Survival—Fiction. 2. Fathers and daughters—Fiction.
3. Camping—Fiction. 4. Islands—Fiction. 5. Baja California
(Mexico)—Fiction.] I. Title.
PZ7.T2186Sw 1994
[Fic]—dc20 93-32435

Designed by Lisa Peters
Map by Rich Knauel
Printed in Hong Kong
A B C D E
A B C D E (pbk.)

For

CAROL AND ROCK THOMPSON

The Island

U.S. Navy Hydrographic Office Sailing Direction, Publication #84—West Coasts of Mexico and Central America, Including the Gulfs of California and Panama—1969—Isla Viernes Dulce (Sweet Friday Island) 29.6 miles off the Mexican mainland, north of Punta Piloto, almost midway between the east and west shores of the Sea of Cortez, 306 feet high at its highest point. It is 1.6 miles long and 0.6 miles wide at extremity, easily recognizable by its guano cliffs. Deep water surrounds it, but shelves and rocks extend outward, exposed only at low tide. Advise extreme caution. A freshwater spring has been reported at the north end but not verified. Several caves are said to be on the west side of the island. Due to tidal movements in this area, use caution in approaching it, especially from the north. There is suitable cove anchorage on the south end for vessels up to four feet draft but not recommended in heavy southwesterly weather. There is a small sandy beach within the protected southern cove for small boat landing. Use caution on an easterly approach to the cove because of rocks with depth of at least two fathoms at high tide. Isla Viernes Dulce, formerly part of Rancho Sweet Friday, the Spanish land grant that once stretched from Crucero la Trinidad south to Punta Fermin, is uninhabited.

Sweet
Friday
Island

CHAPTER ONE
Saturday Morning

DAWN HAD BARELY BRUSHED California with soft pinks and yellows that cool April Saturday when my father drove the shining new Toyota Land Cruiser up in front of the Crescent Way condo. His headlights raked the neat cul-de-sac. White shafts pierced the low-lying mist that made Laguna Beach ghostly.

Weeks of waiting were over, and I scooped up a faded red sleeping bag plus a battered old suitcase packed for seven days. I said a hurried good-bye to my mother, made a quick check to see that I had my wallet and ID, then ran down the stairs two at a time, the door banging behind me in the morning hush.

We were Mexico bound—a-camping we would go.

Standing at the back of the Cruiser, clad in scuffed high-tops, faded jeans, and an ancient brown navy jacket, a yellow Caterpillar tractor cap on his curly head, a grinning Samuel J. Toland kissed my cheek, bear-hugged me, and said, "Hi, baby," tossing my belongings unceremoniously inside.

That was his style, always casual.

Strapped on the Toyota roof were a Mercury outboard motor and a big green bag containing an inflatable boat, a British Avon Redshank.

To salty sea we would go, then on to an exotic island.

"Hi, Pop," said I, returning his affection and bear hug. He was easy to love.

Then we rolled.

The odor of his pipe smoke, rich and sweet with apple- and honey-flavored Dutch tobacco, was already heavy inside the vehicle. That smell was always a part of him, indoors or out. An old-fashioned man in many ways, he allowed himself three smokes a day but often had that stained pipe clamped, cold, between his teeth.

No, my mother wasn't joining us.

And the idea of my going off to Mexico with my "old man" wasn't unanimously approved of, by any means. Mother didn't approve of it for several reasons. My boyfriend, Stevie, who had tickets to a Crosby, Stills, and Nash concert at Long Beach Civic that week, didn't like it for even more reasons. "Who wants to go anywhere, any-time, with their old man?" he snorted.

Well, I did. I had a feeling we wouldn't be doing this kind of thing many more times. I'd be going off to college in two years.

Elizabeth and Sam Toland? Well, they'd been divorced six years, and little had changed in all that time. I dearly loved them both, but they were still at fierce and declared war and would be until death did them part. I'd learned to live with that smoldering war. Almost, not quite. Yet I knew they were much better off singly.

I was barely nine when the court awarded custody to my mother. But Mr. Samuel J. Toland had seldom disappointed me, and we were as close as the situation allowed. In those days, I saw him almost weekly and always looked forward to my times with him, was always a little sad when he delivered me back home. We had fun.

Of course, after I turned twelve, I often took the bus over to his apartment, which was in a nearby town. Though he'd been on the brink of it several times, S. J. had never remarried. The right lady hadn't come along, he claimed—likely one who wanted to goof around in the mountains or deserts every weekend. Or go island hopping. Secretly, I was glad. I wanted him for myself. A twelve-year-old daughter can be possessive.

By the time I turned fifteen, which occurred two months and two weeks before we went to Mexico, the relationship was closer than ever. He shared his innermost thoughts with me, and no one could have asked for much more than that. My father was always my special hero.

He grinned over. "You're sure not taking much, Peg-eye."

My name is Margaret Anne Toland, but he usually called me Peg, Peggy, Peg-eye; very occasionally, Maggie Anne.

"I don't think I need much where we're going, do I?"

He laughed. "You sure as shootin' don't."

Usually he had a quick and easy laugh. Civil engineer, super salesman of tractors, backhoes, earth-movers, and such, he was a lean, wiry, perpetually sunburned man with a narrow face and large, expressive blue eyes. The sandy, curly hair was slowly turning whitish gray. Pushing fifty, he was wrinkling up, too, in a nice weathered way. Any daughter of fifteen would have been pleased with his looks. So much for that.

Exactly where we were going was the Sea of Cortez, also known as the Gulf of California, the long body of water between Baja, or Lower California, and Mexico proper.

Why we were going was nothing more or less

than vacation and father-daughter exploration. I'd been exploring with him for years—before and after Big D, old devil Divorce—either by the Sierra Nevada trout streams or down in Mexico, once in Alaska. I'd learned a lot from S. J. Toland and was as good as any camper around. He loved it and so did I.

Sometimes we had memory time: *You remember that time in Alaska when the bear . . . ? Remember that July in Nevada when it snowed? Remember Rios Tres when I tipped the canoe?*

Having seen Isla Viernes Dulce—pronounced "EES-la vee-ER-ness DOOL-say," meaning "Sweet Friday Island" in Spanish—on the Cortez chart, in a place where no noisy dune buggy or motorbike could ever lay tracks, we figured to get out there with the rubber boat, something we wouldn't have to tow across the rugged Mexican desert. We'd been planning the trip for months.

Long ago, before another trip, I'd read up on the Cortez in a Sunset book by a man named Cannon. The great San Andreas Fault, the earthquake maker that constantly rattled California with little tremors we often couldn't feel, had hacked off part of Mexico ten or fifteen million years ago. A chasm was neatly cut for the Pacific Ocean to flow into, leaving the narrow Baja peninsula, six or seven hundred miles long, dotted with mountains and deserts. So Isla Viernes Dulce was nothing more than a rectangular mountaintop sticking up out of the Cortez.

"Hey, we're going to have an island all to ourselves," my father said, happily smiling over at me as we roared along.

Without much doubt, he'd missed his calling in life. He should have been a professional explorer, climbed Mount Everest—Sir Samuel Toland; been the first man on the moon—Neil Armstrong Toland.

"You forget anything?" I asked.

"Why, I certainly did," he said cheerfully.

Though he was an expert organizer and always made out a careful list, he usually missed something.

"First-aid kit?"

"Got it."

"Snake-bite kit?"

"Absolutely."

"Plenty of water?"

"Plenty. Twelve gallons."

"Camera?"

"Yep!"

"Enough insulin?"

He nodded.

Unfortunately, my father was an insulin-dependent diabetic, needing two injections every day, and that always worried Mother when we went away on these wilderness trips. But he was very careful, watching what he ate and drank. Though he never minded talking about his problem, he'd become furious if someone said he shouldn't do something, shouldn't go somewhere. He could spout off the names of pro football players or baseball players who had diabetes; other famous people like Thomas Edison, Ernest Hemingway, Mary Tyler Moore, Spencer Tracy—dozens of others who had lived full lives. Most of the time he truly acted as if the illness didn't exist. I seldom thought about it.

"T.P.?" I asked.

He looked over at me archly. "Yes, Peg. I brought six rolls of high-grade toilet paper. One a day. Enough to cover the island, almost."

I laughed.

He swung smartly out onto Pacific Coast Highway in early, thin traffic and headed south, building speed.

I looked behind me. The Cruiser was crammed, layered to the very roof with coolers, fishing rods, and all manner of gear—boxes of food, jugs of water, gasoline. Even an extra propeller. The rear window was blotted out.

We needed to be self-sufficient on Sweet Friday.

He glanced over and tapped my knee. "Good to have you here, Dodder," he said, smiling blue eyes telling me he meant it.

I nudged his shoulder affectionately. "Good to be here, Pop." I meant that, too.

I couldn't help but think how very nice it would be if he and my mother had been able to get along. The three of us going places and having fun together. A family. Same old impossible dream.

He went on, not thinking of that at all. "Islands are irresistible, Peg. Especially those in tropic waters, but even those in cold water. I've seen them up in New England with stands of pine and fir right down to the rocks. Lobster country."

I nodded, coming to earth. That divorce had been as final as a firecracker bang.

We drummed steadily south under the rising sun and finally swerved by San Diego, turning sharply east to go through El Cajon and a lot of little towns that parallel the Mexican border. Soon the land changed, and the towns gave way to rolling hills as we passed tanker trucks and semis on their way to Arizona.

The day remains vivid, and I can still see myself sitting in the Land Cruiser as we whipped along—a girl nearly physically mature at fifteen, five feet five, with honey-colored hair a shade darker than her father's, athletic enough to hold her own on most occasions. I suppose I was your typical Southern California "beach girl," and I could even surf a little.

I think I knew who Peg Toland was and had a fair amount of self-confidence. But looking back now, remembering it all too well, I did have some unspoken doubts about this safari into the Cortez.

Baja itself, a harsh land of unforgiving deserts and craggy red-black volcanic peaks, a strange land of cactus that leapt at you and of "boojum" trees with spiny tentacles, had sometimes frightened me when I camped down there with S. J. Toland at the age of six. We'd driven the Cuesta del Infierno, the "Grade to Hell," on the road between San Ignacio and the Cortez. Bouncing around while hanging on to the Jeep, I thought I might get lockjaw from gritting my teeth.

The beautiful Cortez was also a strange sea: islands that disappeared at high tide, then erected themselves, dripping and misty, at low tide; great walls of water called "tidal bores" that rushed up channels; deadly wars between fishes, birds, and sea monsters that turned the blue surface red with blood; fearsome and bewitched places where cries of anguish were heard as demons charged down island slopes at night. For centuries there had been Cortez cannibals, maybe the last on earth, Seri Indians with red, white, and purple paint on their noses and cheekbones. They'd lived on Tiburon Island and had barbecued hapless fishermen. Or cooked them in a pot, Cannon had written. The Seris were peaceful now.

But I'd kept all those doubts to myself so as not to disappoint Samuel J. Toland. I owed him that.

Finally, in midmorning, we arrived at Calexico, an American border town, and crossed into Mexicali, the Baja city, pausing long enough for a snack and cold drinks. My father always had midmorning and midafternoon snacks and orange juice on these trips, part of the miserable-and-unending diabetic control. He also had raisins or LifeSavers or sugar cubes handy, just in case he needed a swift shock of sugar in his blood.

We were off again, setting course on Mexico 2, Camino Diablo, the old "Devil's Highway," heading southeast inside the border, and the land quickly became to his liking, if not exactly mine—sparse of people and buildings. The brown men in straw hats trudging along the road looked as if they'd come out of nowhere and were going back to nowhere. They turned their heads and waved if we waved; caught the hot blast from our Toyota engine. Then they dissolved into desert shimmer.

On my father's face was his wilderness smile.

I tuned the radio to a Mexicali station, and that song that sounds like "Wawn-tawn-a-maro," with deep, chiming marimbas, and that one that goes "Kook-a-rook-a-roo," the song of the cuck-oo, came with us far past the bridge over the Colorado River and the sharp turn westward at a place in the road called Rijo. It was just a name on a rock. There were no buildings or people.

As we began to cross the Gran Desierto, the "Grand Desert," toward the waters of the Cortez, bumping along the sand ruts in four-wheel drive, it did seem as if we might drop off the end of the earth.

Though it was at least eighty degrees inside the bucking Toyota, I distinctly remember that I suddenly shivered and didn't know why.

To this day, I remember that icy shudder. Premonition. *Kook-a-rook-a-roo*.

CHAPTER TWO
Saturday Afternoon

"THERE 'TIS," SHOUTED my father, finger arrowed dead ahead through the dusty, vibrating windshield of the Land Cruiser.

So it was. Isla Viernes Dulce sat in a sea of gold as we rounded a last curve of the trail— beefy, deep-notched tires throwing sand. The Toyota crashed along like a fast bulldozer, front wheels pounding carelessly.

I looked at Sweet Friday Island through the powdery glaze of dust. From far away, it was mysterious but inviting, a mound of gray-blue on the horizon. Not much sugary about it.

Beyond it, and to the south, was the brownish white tip of Roca Consaq, "Ship Rock." Farther on south were other islands, some with red-and-black lava tongues, according to the guidebooks. Black volcanic craters sat in many of the islands, clashing with the white of salt flats below. Generally, we knew what was down there but hadn't specifically checked out the others. Waste of time, we'd thought, since we'd settled on Sweet Friday.

"Awful small," I said.

"We're thirty miles from it. Wait'll you get close." He was grinning widely with anticipation.

Turning sharp south, we began to bump on down to Boca de Cangrejo, "Mouth of the Crab," a little village that most Mexican maps ignored. It sat on a quarter-mile of beach, sand rising gently to the few meager houses. Shacks, really. I counted eight.

Finally we drew up in front of the cantina, the village store. The Cortez shore guide, our bible, said the store had limited supplies for fishermen and was operated by a man named Raul Clemente.

A gas pump hung its broken head in the sun directly in front of the cantina, and I saw that it was sitting on concrete blocks, hooked to nothing, totally useless. We didn't need gas, anyway.

Peering around, my father said, "Not New York City, is it?"

Hardly, though I'd never been to NYC.

But Boca de Cangrejo finally acknowledged us with dog yelps and a few cautious children with thin legs and tentative toes coming out of sagging doorways, moving into the single street, just a vague space, keeping a bashful distance.

I said hello to them. They didn't answer. Just stared.

Women moved out into the sapphire light, stony faced but probably not meaning to be. At the far end of the houses, a chubby, straw-hatted man stood by an outboard motor on a wooden stand. He studied us briefly, then bent again.

Between the houses and the high-tide mark, a few fishing skiffs were pulled up at this hour. Now, over low mud flats and glistening sandbars and thin pools of water, the glassy Cortez was lapping inward. An onshore breeze picked up the damp smell and socked it to the village.

"Is this really picturesque?" asked my father, eyebrows raised. The guidebook had described it that way.

"I guess." I was not really concerned about the village, only about the island. At sea level, it looked so very far away, and I wondered how our fabric boat would do on the trip out.

A man who might have been forty, or abouts, had suddenly filled the doorway of the cantina to examine us, though not with unfriendliness. There was an animal's curiosity in his eyes. Skin reddish brown, hair shiny black, precisely cut and precisely combed. He was rather tall and thin, crisp jeans going up his legs from cowboy boots. White shirt spotless, he was an immaculate man; even his boots were mirrored, with polish. Was this Raul Clemente? He was handsome.

My father got out of the Toyota, removing the pipe from his teeth. *"Buenos días, señor."*

I alighted, too, feeling alien here.

My father went on in pidgin Spanish. "That's a rough trail back there. *Muy malo.*" I knew that meant "very bad."

The tall man nodded.

Behind him, the cantina was like a cave, appearing dark and cool in its depths. There were no windows in the building. I could hear a radio playing inside—the Beatles' "Strawberry Fields." Maybe the Yuma station or El Centro. But it seemed as if we were a thousand miles from Arizona, a million miles from city coils of concrete.

Lingering eyes were still on us from the houses, and the dogs came warily closer.

My father went on slowly. "We'd like to stay here. *Aquí.* Tonight, señor. *El noche.* Set up camp on the beach." He motioned south because it widened down there. "We'll leave in the morning, señor—is it Clemente? *Vamoose mañana!* We won't bother you. Even be glad to pay you some rent. *Renta!* Okay?"

The handsome man answered in faultless English. "It is all right with me, my friend."

Father stood there foolishly, then laughed.

"Hey, I'm glad you speak English. I just assumed you spoke only Spanish. You know, you're way down in the boonies here, Señor Clemente."

Glancing at me briefly, the tall man said, "I was born on the Arizona border and worked in Somerton for a while. That's near Yuma."

"Oh," said my father, still looking sheepish.

Clemente stared at our loaded Toyota, then sank into the shadows of the store, steel boot taps clicking on tile.

Several of the children had sidled up to me. They whispered softly to each other, occupied with my blond hair—admiring it. I'd combed it out during the last mile to the village and had put a barrette at the nape of my neck, making a brush that hung over the back of my collar.

One little girl touched it; then they all giggled and ran.

I felt strange, having my hair touched. For a few seconds, I longed for the paved street and walks and the shrubbery and nice condos of Crescent Way.

CHAPTER THREE
The Cantina

WE VENTURED ON INSIDE the cantina. Our eyes took a moment to focus. The cantina had adobe's usual pleasant, cool dryness. Odors mingled together, but the store looked clean. Yet it appeared that the owner was letting his stock run down, so that when the shelves were barren, he'd go, too. Maybe it looked that way all the time—big gaps along the rows of goods.

Aging, fly-spattered cans and bottles—mixed American and Mexican labels—were on the shelves behind a single counter, and bags of rice and beans rested on the scrubbed tile. The guidebook said Mexican fishermen, working the area by season, often put in here for food and supplies.

There was also a hamper of curled, salted dried fish. Near it, on a half-barrel, perched an old woman in total black, eyes watery and deep in her skull. Her skin was like parchment; her hair, streaked with white, was pulled back severely. Scanning from me to my father, the watery eyes grew wide and began to blaze. They stayed on him, blazing.

Why? I wondered. He'd done nothing. If the saying *If looks could kill* was ever true, he was a dead man. Whew.

The big battery radio on the counter, one of those wide-band jobs that can pick up police and marine signals, was now off "Strawberry Fields" and into a singing commercial for shampoo. Yuma station.

The tall man flicked it off, and the silence of the village rushed in. Except for the faint lap of the Cortez water, there was no sound now. Not even a clock ticking. We were caught in a tile-floored vacuum.

My mouth was parched. I asked, "Anything cold?" We had canned pop-tops in the coolers, but why waste them?

My father said, "Yeah, I'd like a diet drink, too, if you've got one. Sugarless all the way."

Clemente moved to open the rusting butane refrigerator. "Seven-Up. Royal Crown. Coke. No diets."

"Coke for me," I said.

"Seven-Up for me," said my father, tamping a load into his pipe.

The old crone was really working him over with her sunken eyes, hating every inch of him. He saw it and frowned at me. He was mystified but finally shrugged it off. How else do you deal with that?

I wandered around the cantina, just looking, and heard my father say, "I knew I forgot something, Peg. Fire-starter. I even forgot newspapers to start with."

I turned. He was surveying the shelves. Last chance before the island.

A match flared and the Dutch tobacco ignited, and smoke wreathed the yellow Caterpillar cap. The cantina was about to be treated to a new smell.

I moved around. Coils of rope and spools of fishing line were stabbed on cut-off broomsticks on the rear wall. Feathered lures hung there, too.

". . . fire-starter, and we could use some more fishing line. How about three hundred feet of that line for spare? What's that test?"

"Forty pounds," Clemente replied.

"That's stronger than anything we'll catch," my father estimated.

A very pleasant man, it seemed, Mr. Clemente answered, "Oh, be optimistic, señor," and then snagged a can of starter before moving to the back wall. Over his shoulder he said, "I cannot take

19

you myself, since I must go to Mexicali for a few days, but if you'd like to go fishing tomorrow I can arrange for a guide. A very experienced man."

"No, thanks," my father said. "We're going out to the island for a week. Isla Dulce."

Plainly startled, Clemente turned, and his hand fell from the forty-pound test line. His eyes went from my father to the old woman. I swear a look of alarm was exchanged. Then he peered at us again, a tight frown working across his forehead. There was actually a sudden, unexplainable tension in the dark cantina, like that thick hush before a storm's first crack of thunder.

"That is no place to go," said Clemente, each word measured. Fishing line slithered across the spotless floor, hissing over the tile. His hand finally braked the spool.

"Why not?" my father asked, glancing at me and drawing on his pipe.

"You cannot land there. No one can. No one goes there anymore."

"Is it restricted?" my father asked, engineer's mind always working. The Hydrographic Office had said nothing about the island being military land.

Clemente did not answer.

"A game preserve?" my father asked, determined to find out.

The worst mistake anyone could ever make with Samuel J. Toland, earth-mover expert, was to tell him that something couldn't be done or that he, in particular, couldn't do it. He'd stay up all night just to defeat a puzzle.

Again, the tall man didn't answer, but he began looping the fishing line under his elbow, counting in his head, bringing it over his palm to measure it. Each turn showed annoyance. It was as if we'd caught him doing something evil in little, lost Boca.

"Why do you want to go out there?" Clemente finally asked.

My father looked over at me and hooted in pure astonishment.

Why? Well, because the island was there. And we were as harmless a pair, as live-and-let-live a pair of campers as had ever ridden into Boca. We were absolutely not the destructive gringo wanderers playing around in dune buggies. Deep into the conservation kick, we always cleaned up like busy ants, saved our empties, left no garbage behind—even picked up other people's tossings.

"Just to camp," said my father. "Get away from everything. Dune buggies, dirt bikes, people. That's why we came here. No other reason. We could have gone to Percebu, but it's the week before Easter and already crunch time over there."

He nodded at me. "This is my daughter, and I'd never put her into danger. Believe me. No sir. Never."

The tall man cut the line with a sharp movement of his blade and returned to the counter. "That is exactly what I'm talking about. Danger. I'm only thinking of your safety. It cannot be safely approached, and those waters are filled with sharks."

Subject closed! Over and out! Clemente began to scratch figures on a piece of torn brown bag.

We were stunned. Here we'd driven over three hundred miles. Crossed brutal desert. Bought all that food. Got boat and engine ready to go. *Set your mind on something and* pow, *it's shot down.*

But S. J. Toland of Costa Mesa, California, wasn't about to give up. "The Hydrographic Office said it could be approached with caution. I can show you."

Dark eyes lifted from the brown paper bag.

"Is that correct?" my father asked.

Once again, Clemente didn't answer. He just studied his customer, unable to convince this stubborn gringo.

"Correct?" my father repeated.

Of course, he was certain he was right. Great

care was taken with those government navigational publications. Lives depended on them. The navy had said there was that protected cove and beach on the south end. True, we knew the currents rushed around the island, rising and falling over fifteen feet on a full moon in winter; and if you were caught in a big wind, a Cortez *chubasco*, you could lose your boat as well as your spine on the wave-pounded cliff bottom. We'd also read that the current sweeping past the island could be savage, becoming a tidal bore when it reached the Colorado River entry and making the river run backward for half an hour. But if you timed it, and had a good motor, there should be no trouble, as my father had maintained long ago.

He now insisted to Clemente, "There's a safe landing on the south end if you go in at high water and be careful."

Clemente then spoke to the old woman, and she answered in a half minute of hoarse speech. We had no idea what she was saying, but he nodded frequently, agreeing with her.

After she finished, he said to us, changing his attitude abruptly—even smiling, relaxed again— "I'm very sorry. That landing is gone now. The hurricane, the one that destroyed San Felipe and almost destroyed us, sucked it out. There is nothing but a steep rock face now." He nodded toward me. "You should definitely not take the pretty señorita there."

The crone swiveled toward us, and her agreeing head, a leather block with high Indian cheekbones, went up and down like one of those toy birds that drink water endlessly. She *did* understand some English. I think she understood every word.

Turning to me, my father said, "Well, Maggie Anne, how do you like these advisories of good joy? If we listen to them, we have just lost our enchanted island, our special Bali Hai."

As a matter of pure fact, I was again having mixed feelings about it, anyway. They'd been creeping in since the desert. There were a lot of nice mainland beaches on down the coast, the guidebook said. . . .

But the Missouri mule tried one last time. "Señor Clemente," he said, as if starting out to prove the world was flat, "have you been out there lately to look at that cove? Sand usually comes back. The tide brings it in. Mother Nature at work. You know that."

"Señor," Clemente soothed, his patience stretching, "there is no use to go out there. It has always been dangerous. No one goes near it. And believe me, it is not a lovely, enchanted island. It is very rough and dry on top, home to snakes and lizards. And more shark fins than I have fingers circle it all the time."

The cantina keeper seemed one hundred percent sincere. I certainly believed him.

But Samuel J. Toland manufactured a very false and disappointed sigh, one that I had heard in other places, at other times. "Well, Peggy, I guess that's out. We'll look at islands south of here in the morning."

"Yes, that's best." Clemente smiled widely.

"Any suggestions?" my father asked blandly. Yet I saw that his head was cocked defiantly; agitation showed around his lips. It was a veiled expression, but I knew it well: *I double-dare you.*

"Yes, señor, Isla Piño, a beautiful and safe island for you and your daughter, forty miles south of here by sea. Longer by road."

My father continued to smile falsely, though Clemente would never have known. "Isla Piño it is," he announced.

I felt hollow.

"Ah, good," said Clemente, obviously relieved.

My father paid for the drinks, the starter, and the forty-pound test line. Then we went out into the bright light again, my father knocking spent tobacco into the fine white sand of the street.

Standing in front of the cantina, looking over

at Sweet Friday, he said softly, "I don't believe one cotton-picking word of it. Maybe he's growing pot out there. Cortez Golden."

"He seemed sincere."

My father shrugged.

As we went toward the Land Cruiser, I said, "Did you see that old woman looking at you? She hated you. Why?"

"I saw. I don't know why."

As he put his hand on the Toyota door, he said, angrily and stubbornly, "Dammit, Peg, I'm not running away."

He really meant, *We're not running away.*

I looked out over the glittering afternoon sea at the awash box of Isla Viernes Dulce, now hazy around the base, and for the second time that day I felt as if a cold hand had touched the warm flesh of my back.

CHAPTER FOUR

Saturday Night

BY NINE O'CLOCK, Boca de Cangrejo became as silent as a graveyard, and not a sliver of light could be seen from any of the huts or the cantina. But the stars over the Cortez chased away the reality of the village, painting over the poverty with thin silver.

We talked quietly in the tent, in our sleeping bags, first about Raul Clemente and the old crone, then about the dark sea that sheeted out in front of us. Earlier, before going to bed, we'd seen a shrimper working on the south horizon. At least, my father thought it was a shrimp boat.

I think he realized that I was uneasy, especially after what Clemente had said, and he tried to calm my unspoken fears without acknowledging them. He'd been under fire in World War II many times and knew what fear was.

"Just remember what I said a long time ago:

we both use common sense. If we're collecting wood, we throw some rocks into the brush to chase the rattlers, if there are any." The guidebook said the Baja region had ten different varieties. "If we're going through cholla, dodge around the type that jumps." The guidebook said you have to use pliers to jerk out the spines. Also check shoes and bedding for scorpions. They like to hide.

"We don't have to worry about animals. None can survive—no food for them. Just iguanas, and they're about as vicious as rabbits."

They certainly looked vicious!

"We'll go swimming, won't we?" I asked.

"Absolutely."

"Cannon said there were a lot of sharks around."

"He's right, but the chances of a shark biting are about the same as of you getting hit on the Coast Highway by a covered wagon. Almost all of them take off if you come flapping their way. Even the hammerheads would rather eat a giant grouper than you." He grinned and added, "I think."

I hope so, I thought.

There was a silence—a thoughtful one, so far as I was concerned. Then I asked, "Why is the Cortez so strange?"

"I haven't the faintest and Cannon doesn't say why, either. And he's the expert. But I'll admit it is strange compared to other seas."

Long ago he'd told me he spent two months, before he married Mother, knocking around the Cortez, fishing and exploring. I remembered him telling me about the Encantados, the enchanted islands well south of us. Rocks fell off them and floated. *Floating rocks!* They were pumice, a spongy form of volcanic glass. He'd told me that, sailing eastward, he'd often see mirages well after the islands had disappeared—suddenly they'd appear at full height. Strange, he'd said. Yes.

I'd first seen the boojum trees on that camping trip in Baja when I was six. They looked like big wax tapers, telephone poles with thousands of tiny daggers on them, and with grotesque wiry tentacles at the top, strange feelers, moving only in a strong breeze. The real name for them is *cirio*, but a botanist gave them the common name after the creature in Lewis Carroll's poem *The Hunting of the Snark*.

On that first trip I'd also seen the *cardones*, the world's tallest cactus, reaching up to sixty or seventy feet; and barrel cactus, which some people said stored fresh water. I was no stranger to the strangeness of the land, but I also remembered the nightmare I had after we returned. I dreamed I was lost among those weird boojums with their spiny antennae.

S. J. Toland was always exploring. Even that day, as we drove on toward the Cortez, he'd taken a detour southeast of Mexicali to show me some mud volcanos. They were bubbling mud pots, about waist high. They made a deep, wet burping sound. We seemed to be standing in a bizarre lunar garden, and I was happy to leave it.

After another long silence, I asked, "Are all the people down here like Señor Clemente and that old lady?"

He laughed. "People are people, anywhere. We're all different."

I said, "I hope we don't meet any more like them." I could still see the old crone's eyes hating my father, someone she'd just met. Pure hatred.

"The only people we might meet, but I doubt very much we will, are *vagabundos del mar,* 'sea gypsies.' They sometimes stop on islands to over-night it. I've seen their tiny campfires."

"Sea gypsies?" I said, frowning at him in the faint light from the tent opening.

"Men who roam around the Cortez. They're lonely but like it that way. They don't ask any favors of anyone. They travel in beat-up canoes with their fishing gear and their shark spears, a couple of cooking pots, some wine bottles filled with water. The only reason they go ashore in places like Boca is for beans, tortillas, and chile peppers."

"What a way to live," I said.

My father laughed again. "Maybe not. I think I could be a *vagabundo del mar*. I get fed up with civilization every now and then."

I already knew that.

Finally he said, "Let's get some sleep. You're going to have the time of your life for the next week, Peg-eye."

"Is that a promise?"

"That's a promise." He rolled over with a yawning "Good night."

It had been a long day, and I soon fell asleep.

CHAPTER FIVE

Sunday Morning

FRESH SUN BEHIND US, Sea of Cortez sparkling all the way to the horizon, we rode down on Sweet Friday Island, its east cliffs shining with marbled gray-white guano. The bird lime was splashed around like sundae topping, and there appeared to be a noisy wing-and-feather convention over there.

"Pelicans! Cormorants! Gulls! Jeeze-Louise, I see some black oyster catchers and a stilt!" my father shouted, scanning along the cliffs. He was in explorer's heaven.

The lazy sea sent white spray against the base of the island, washing over a shelf that appeared to extend irregularly down the entire east side. There was movement all over it.

"Sea lions," yelled my father, pointing excitedly.

We couldn't hear their joyful dawn bellowing

because of the Mercury engine's whine, but my father shouted to them, *"Buenos días,"* anyway. *Good morning,* sea lions! What a super day!

Big boulders and rock slabs had tumbled down from the cliff walls and now rested on the shelf, which would be high out of the water by ten feet or so at low tide. "Peg-eye, there's a veritable feast of sea life on that thing, I'd bet. I can't wait to walk it. Tide pools. Wow!" He was so excited. So boyish. So young again.

I was glad we'd come out.

We'd talked about sharks, Clemente having said they constantly circled the island; so, nearing it, we kept a lookout for the dusky triangular fins. Thus far we had seen none. Big relief. Wrong, Señor Clemente!

And now Isla Viernes Dulce sat there in the yellow light, volleying sound back to us. The high-pitched chatter of the Mercury caromed off its walls and returned to almost deafen us. But with all that racket, no human came running to the edge to peer down on us between the clumps of mesquite and creosote bushes. So the navy had been right about Sweet Friday being uninhabited. We'd have it all to our exclusive selves.

I yelled, "We have our own special island!"

S. J.'s smile at me was prairie wide as he nodded agreement.

We'd left a note, to which fifty pesos were pinned, on the windshield of the Toyota: *Dear Mr. Clemente—We took your advice and have gone to Isla Piño for the week. Please look after the Land Cruiser. Thank you. Sincerely, Sam Toland.*

"Rugged," he yelled, craning his head upward, eyes dancing with challenge.

Yes, it was. I was glad we'd brought our hiking boots. Up there was no place for tennies.

We knew there was cactus in the granite crevices—the chollas with their fuzzy, fingerlike arms; the ocotillos with their long feelers; maybe miniature smoke and elephant trees. We were too far north in the Cortez for the boojums. It always bothered my father if he couldn't name off the trees and plants wherever we went—Sam Toland, the curious botanist.

The twelve-foot Avon Redshank had been performing beautifully. There wasn't a better inflatable anywhere, according to its captain. Constructed of heavy-duty nylon, coated with something called Hypalon, it had been designed for British commando use. With a beam of over five feet, the silver craft had two inflatable compartments.

"You can puncture half of it, fold it back, and still float nicely on the other half. I'm not worried about the good Redshank," he'd said when we planned the trip.

We drummed by the busy, noisy shelf about fifty yards out, then laid a wide, churned circle, avoiding the string of rocks at the southeast end. Finally he nodded inland.

Then I saw the cove, behind an entrance about thirty yards wide, enlarging inside like a giant soup spoon. A fine lip of white sand broke up the rocks directly opposite the cove entrance, just as the Hydrographic Office had described it.

"Would you look at that beach!" I yelled. "Wow!"

"And that cantina guy is a dirty liar," father Toland yelled back, crowing with delight. "Just look at that sand. Washed away in a hurricane? Phooey! Hey, it's sensational."

Maybe 150 feet long and 50 deep, the sand lip sloped inward from the steep high-tide mark. At low tide, the bottom would probably be exposed downhill all the way to the cove entrance, like a levee. Brown-and-black lava cliffs rose again sharply from the beach, but they looked as if they could be climbed without too much trouble, especially on the east side. Rocks flanked the little beach on either side and paraded on east around to the beginning of the shelf. There was a million dollars' worth of privacy in that bowl.

My father shouted, "This is as pretty a cove as you'll ever see. You could rip this out of the *National Geographic* in full color."

He set a course splitting the mouth, and we skimmed toward the cove, riding down on what little incoming tide was left. We slugged away for about three minutes and then swept through the entrance, engine banging sharply in the still bowl, noise climbing up the cliff ahead and folding back.

Then the Mercury was cut and jerked up, and the Redshank grounded smoothly a moment later, producing that pleasing swish on wet sand.

Father said smugly to me, "Dodder, we have just done it."

True. So safe had been this voyage that I hopped out of the British commando boat without getting a drop of water on my feet. So much for Raul Clemente of Boca de Cangrejo and his dire prediction of disaster.

We looked around the beach and cliffs, listening for the bird and sea lion echoes. Not too many people would understand why two humans would want to spend a vacation here. Some people would say, Why go on holiday where there are no lights, no music, no entertainment, no other human beings? But then, of course, some people enjoy high rises, traffic noise, and jammed freeways, and aren't bothered by bad air. Or so they say.

With the engine stilled, we became aware of the many different sounds of Isla Viernes Dulce —the slight crooning breeze; the sloshing low thud of the small rollers as they hit the east side; the water lapping gently at the edge of the beach in the cove; the birdsong; even the coughing, *aarpp*-ing sea lion calls—Sweet Friday symphony.

I felt very lazy. "It's so beautiful down here, Pops. So very peaceful. I may want to stay forever. Just listen." Sea-gypsy privacy.

"All right, we've got five whole days to listen after we set up camp. Work, then play."

There is never any fun in breaking camp but there is always deep pleasure in setting it up, finding the exact right places to pitch the tent, dig the fire pit, make a table of sorts, scrounge around to see what can be used for homey touches. With an eye toward convenience and protection, Father selected a spot near the rock overhang on the east side of the cliff, up on the beach about forty feet from the high-tide line, figuring we could put the two-gallon thermos of water and the five extra two-gallon supermart plastic bottles under the rock ledge. The boat engine and anything else dew might attack would also go under there.

This was all routine to me, veteran of so many camps. The two cooler boxes went there, too, along with firewood planks we'd brought. Suitcase, clothes, food, fire-starter, T.P., books, camera, binoculars would all do better inside the floored dome tent. We'd never use it for sleeping, anyway, unless it rained. Little chance of that in the Cortez in April.

The overhang of rock, jutting out from the cliff base, was about fifteen feet long, projecting out over the sand about five feet, the rock ceiling slanting in at about a twenty-degree angle. Perfect for shelter. Undoubtedly, the current had been carving it out for centuries. It wasn't high enough to stand under but was a good stoop space and storage shelter. We'd also sleep under it in the bags. Perfect.

While the smooth Cortez sparkled outside, the next hour in Sweet Friday cove, with the sun sliding steadily across it chasing dampness, was very busy. I fetched pots and pans and food out of the Redshank while my father erected the tent. Next he hauled the trusty Mercury up and pushed it deep beneath the rock ledge, covering it with the tent bag. Then he pulled the nylon boat higher up on the beach so that no "robber tide" could strand us.

Meanwhile I was rigging that which no worthy

camp can do without—a clothesline. Potty area was designated far to the west, over behind a big rock, with the required shovel. It was adequate coed johnny space, better than most.

But it was while I was putting the finishing touches on my labors, digging the fire pit, that I first felt eyes. My back was to the cliff, and suddenly eyes were boring into my head, just above the neck. I felt them.

Of course, this happens now and then to everyone. You're sitting in a restaurant or walking around or driving down the freeway; you become aware that eyes are on you; you turn and the person usually glances away, caught in the common act of spying.

I stopped shoveling and turned, looking up at the cliff top. I saw nothing, beast nor human.

Yet the eyes didn't go away. They speared me steadily.

I called over, quietly as I could, "Daddy, I think someone, or something, is watching us."

Near the overhang, he straightened, frowning at me. "From where?"

"Up there." I pointed.

"From where up there, Peggy?" he asked impatiently. He was never one to deal in abstracts.

"I'm not sure. I just feel eyes on us. Right now." My throat was suddenly tight with fear. Fear grew, also, in my stomach.

He came over near me, laughing and shouting. "Hey, you up there, quit your snooping! Hey, lizard, close your eyes, you're spooking my daughter."

"I'm not kidding," I said. My stomach tickled.

He shook his head. "I can't see anything, Peg." He reached down, picked up a rock, and heaved it toward the top of the cliff. Falling short, it tumbled back to the beach. "Now, you feel better?"

I half nodded. I didn't feel better at all.

He saw that immediately and said, "Might have been an animal."

I kept looking. The eyes were still there, I believed. Somewhere. I wasn't making them up.

About fifty feet high, though not all sheer, the cliff face to the cove was uneven, gouged out in places by small slides. Crusts seemed about to break off. Clinging to the scant soil, full of pebbles, were a few clumps of coarse green brush with fuzzy white stalks. There were also a few trails of cactuslike plants with long creepers.

My father snorted his disbelief and took my hand, as he'd done so many times when I was a little girl and desperately afraid of thunderstorms. He walked me back to the edge of the retreating water. "Look, Peg," he ordered. "There's nothing there. See?"

From this larger view, the cliff face above the beach resembled the backside of an earthen dam, with compacted soil and strata of rock. He said, "Come on, baby, look hard. Nothing is up there unless it's a big iguana. Cool that imagination."

I looked. Side to side. Up and down. I couldn't see a blessed thing, either. "But I swear eyes were on us."

"Would you like to go up?"

"Guess not. I'd rather go swimming."

"You always did have a good imagination." He sighed and walked back to camp, the overhang now being headquarters.

I finished the fire pit without further comment.

He called over, "Swimming now, and then we'll go fishing this afternoon in the boat. Catch us some bass for dinner. Okay?"

"Terrific."

CHAPTER SIX
Midmorning

I CHANGED IN THE TENT and then waited outside while he pulled on his ancient denim trunks, patched by his own hand. Then we raced to the water like old times, and I beat him by ten feet, doing a pelican's belly-whopper. I was far the better swimmer, but he wasn't too bad for a gracefully aging man. Truthfully, he was in pretty good shape for a half-century on earth.

Well, it couldn't have been any finer, any nicer, any sweeter on that fresh Sunday morn in the south cove of old, uninhabited Isla "Friday" Dulce. Though we hadn't forgotten about the shark warning, and weren't likely to, we just didn't talk about that upsetting possibility. We ignored the jaws as if they didn't exist.

The water was warm but not too warm, and we swam on outside the cove entrance until we could feel the strong pull of the ebbing tide. It swept around the island on both sides and then joined in a frothy rip about a hundred yards south, on an angle from the eastern string of rocks. We'd end up in La Paz if we got into that boiling rip, so we reversed course and stroked slowly back into the spoon of sheltering water.

Once, we stopped to tread awhile and rest. He sputtered, "You think this is tide?" spurting water like a whale.

"What else could it be?"

"Wrong. They call it tide, but this sea doesn't have a real tide of its own. This is all lift from the Pacific. What is three or four feet down at La Paz funnels up here and becomes ten or fifteen feet, depending on the moon. Isn't that wild? You know how fast this water can go? Twenty miles an hour. Like a millrace."

"Where'd you learn all that, Old Man?"

He grinned, tapped his head like an old scholar would, and began swimming again.

Ashore, I'm sure the globe was rotating around as usual; church bells were ringing all over the land. My mother was probably reading the Sunday *L.A. Times,* as usual, on quiet Crescent Way, but out here we were doing something very special, unknown to anyone—owning our own island for a carefree week.

Reaching the shallows ahead of him, I stood,

feeling marvelous, refreshed. I whisked the water out of my eyes, shook it out of my hair, banged a clogged eardrum, and waited for him. He was kicking up to the beach like a slow Mississippi paddleboat. After he thrashed on up, we walked out, puffing and panting, ready to flop onto the warm sand.

To that point, we certainly hadn't been paying any particular attention to the beach, but I think we both saw what had happened to the Redshank at the same instant.

My father, I remember so clearly, gasped, "Good God! Oh, my good God!"

The inflatable, midway to the blue dome tent, was almost flat, yet we both knew it had been fully inflated when we went out to swim. Those valves were foolproof—this was a commando boat, after all, tough as hippo hide—yet the poor hull lay on the sand like a wrinkled, grotesque, popped balloon.

"You open those valves, Peg?" he yelled, running for the boat.

"Me open them?" I was running, too.

That boat was our only connection to the mainland.

In a few seconds, we looked down in shock on the invincible British boat. It now had the appearance of a strange, slaughtered animal, a beached Hypalon sea monster that had been gutted and would soon rot and smell.

That boat hadn't just exploded from pressure there in the sun. It had been carefully worked over. Someone—some fiend, some breathing *thing*—had ripped the sides and stabbed the bottom. Sweet Friday Island wasn't so sweet after all.

The jolt of fear I'd felt before we went swimming now came back as a sword, making my knees weak, my mouth suddenly dry.

We knelt down in the sand.

The slashes in the fabric were six inches to a foot long and went around both sides, both air compartments. Sliced flaps of nylon, in **V**-shaped slits, extended to the sand from the floor of the boat. No animal had made those. Only a very sharp knife, wielded with a sick vengeance, could have mutilated the compartments. Whoever had done it had even slit the life-preserver seats.

There *had* been someone up on that cliff looking down on us. Those spearing eyes weren't invented by me.

"My God, who would do a vicious thing like this?" my father asked, slowly scanning the cliff top.

Now he knew an overactive female teenage imagination hadn't been manufacturing eyes.

"I don't believe it," he said numbly.

We're trapped, I thought.

My father muttered, "That's two thousand dollars' worth of useless cloth." But it was the deed, not the money, that stunned us.

I looked again toward the cliff top. Mid-morning sun beat down on it, lighting every bush and crevice. If anyone was still up there, watching, *he* was well hidden.

My father got up from his knees and carefully walked all around the pile of Redshank to look for footprints aside from our own. None were visible, but another type of calling card was there. Going back toward the rocks and cliffs—and approaching what appeared to be the best access to the beach—was a long, furrowed drag mark, as if someone had belly-crawled across to the boat and then over toward the tent and back out. In the middle of the dragged area were two half circles gouging the sand; they might have been made by shoe tips dragging along. Then there were pockets that might have been where his elbows dug down.

I had a flashing thought, a quick visual of him sculling along in the sand on his belly, knife in one hand.

"No animal, for sure," said my father bleakly.

I suppose we'd both still been hoping for that,

though no known animal could ever have slashed the boat that way. And if this happened to be an unknown animal, it was one we didn't want to meet.

The access from the cliff to the beach was a steep, natural crawlway of dirt and gravel ending in a big, flat rock that made a natural step. We went over there and looked all around it, finding a single heavy bootprint, as if he'd put all his weight down in the sand on one leg. And either he went back that same way or he went around to walk the shelf, which was now out of water in ebbing tide.

"That's obviously where he came down," said my father, scanning up the crawlway, "and that's a cowboy heel."

Without thinking, I said, "Clemente. He wore cowboy boots. He didn't want us to come here."

"Not the type, and we would have heard his engine coming."

In all the times we'd been camping, nothing like this had ever happened.

My father kept looking down at the bootprint, frowning at it; thinking about it.

I discarded Mr. Clemente, and I remember standing there trying to draw a mental picture, building an entire body from the footprint—a thick-necked, big-bellied white man with long black hair and cold eyes and huge hands and a wet mouth.

"I know what *he* looks like," I said idiotically.

"How the hell do you know what he looks like?" my father shouted. "That's a dumb remark to make." He glared at me.

His anger was flying in all directions. Just as quickly, he apologized. Diabetes doesn't like high stress, and I'm sure blood sugar was on his mind not long after we spotted the slaughtered Redshank. Stress can send the illness out of control. Sweet Friday wasn't a good place for illness of *any* kind.

Suddenly I realized I was standing there in a wisp of bikini. Just from nudity alone, I felt very vulnerable, whether or not *he* was still watching. I crossed my arms over my breasts and ran to the tent and knew immediately that he'd not only looked in but had entered it. There was a sour, stale body odor lingering in the locked-in heat.

In less than ten minutes, he had become an unseen personality in our lives. He'd become someone special on our special island.

I bent down to pick up my clothes and then pulled my hand back, calling out. My sunglasses were now silver-black chips scattered over my clothing and down onto the tent floor. The lenses had been punched out with a knife, and the blade had gone on through, chopping into my bra, panties, and jeans. There were jagged holes in them, matching those on the boat.

I yelled, "Come here and look."

My father came into the tent, face drawn.

"Look. Everything's been stabbed."

He stood motionless, staring down at the pile.

I said, "Daddy, someone was in here trying to kill me. Do you realize that? Someone was sticking a knife into me. That's what this means, doesn't it?"

"I don't know what it means," he said, speaking slowly as if he were in a trance.

That mental picture flashed again. I thought of everything terrible. *Him* jumping down off that flat rock, screaming and running toward us. The knife. Rape. Both of us dead. I pleaded, "Can we fix the boat and leave, Daddy? Right now. I just want to go. Now! I don't want to see him, ever."

"For Lord's sake, I don't want to see him either." Suddenly his hands quivered. Only for a few seconds. But that was scary enough.

"Are you all right?" I asked.

He nodded and seemed to snap out of the trance. "We have to fix the boat."

The repair kit for the Redshank had spare fabric and adhesive. There were also an instruction manual and directions for repairing rips. A child could do it.

"Get dressed, Peg," he said, stepping outside the tent, looking up at the cliff top again.

I had another bra in the suitcase, an extra pair of jeans, and several pairs of panties. I certainly wouldn't wear what *he*'d chopped with his blade. They were soiled and good only for the fire. His image was building again as I dressed, realizing that my own hands were now trembling.

I put on jeans and a shirt, toweled my hair quickly, and knelt down to find my toiletries kit, which I knew I'd placed by the blankets in one corner of the tent. Incredibly, the black bag was gone. I looked everywhere, then went outside.

My father was kneeling down by the hulk, taking a closer look at the rips. He glanced up. "If we get even a half a boat out of this, we can float back to Boca and get help from Clemente, or over to San Felipe, depending on which way we go. The Mexican police should handle this, not us."

Thankfully, he now seemed to be composed, more in control of himself. Shock was wearing off, I guess. He rose. "By the way, where'd you put the ax? It's almost the only weapon we have."

"By the fire pit," I answered.

We looked over there. The bright red handle was gone.

"Great," my father murmured. "Where's the gaff?"

The fishing gaff, about three feet long, had the usual sharp, curved steel hook on the end. It could be a terrible weapon. I looked over to the fishing rods, standing against the cliff. The gaff was gone.

"The guy knows what could hurt him," my father said, blowing out a breath, shaking his head.

I added, "He also took my makeup bag."

"Your makeup bag? What the heck was in there?"

"Usual things. Comb, lipstick, cologne, suntan lotion, face cream, bobby pins, toothbrush . . ."

He shook his head and scanned along the cliff top. "Makeup bag he steals . . ."

Finally, he said, "Let's take a walk down by the water. We need a minute to sort this out. He's really a case."

I went with him.

Standing by the water's edge, far down from the cliff, on the bottom of the cove, my father put his arms around me to say, "Peg, I didn't mean this to happen. You don't know how sorry I am. I'd never put you in jeopardy if I could help it. You know that, don't you?"

I knew it, and I returned his hug, kissed his cheek. In the beginning, months ago, I'd wanted to come out here as much as he had.

Then he held me at arm's length. "I have to be truthful. If you put all this together—slashing the boat, stabbing your clothes, stealing the ax, makeup kit—I think we're mixed up with a very insane man. What he gets out of the makeup kit doesn't mix with the ax or chopping the boat. He might just want to make us leave—not hurt us. So we're going to try and please him. We'll try to get out of here before dark and float over toward San Felipe. I'm not wild about spending the night out there, floating around. We can't use the Merc on half a boat. But I'm not wild about spending the night here, either. Dangerous either way, Peg. Dangerous if we go, dangerous if we stay. But that's a good boat, even half of it. Okay? We go?"

"We go."

"All settled."

I nodded but also asked, "Why is he doing this to us?"

He shook his head. "I haven't the faintest clue. I think maybe stabbing your clothes was thoughtless. Maybe he was angry at your sunglasses. They were staring at him. Who knows? But he's sure nuts, in my opinion. So we'd best get cracking, Peg-eye. Okay?"

I nodded once more as he pulled me to him again. He was more like the father I'd always known. My hero; my protector, adviser. "The worst thing we can do with this crummy goon is to panic."

Again I nodded; but if he'd really known, I was already panicked. So scared I could hardly breathe.

CHAPTER SEVEN
Sunday Afternoon

ABOUT NOON, sitting on the beach by the pile of Hypalon, my father downed a cup of orange juice to keep his system in balance. Then he busied himself, though the kit had been put together with only minor repairs in mind—a gash from sliding over rocks, a puncture from dock timber—not to seal fifty holes.

Nonetheless, he said, "We'll try to fix the stern, then I'll fold and tie back the rest to make a bulkhead for the bow. That'll give us something about six feet long. We'll use the oars and addle out, then drift. The current's going south, and we'll steer for San Felipe or anywhere below. . . ."

That sounded good. With the water going at twenty miles an hour, it wouldn't take us long to veer toward shore.

"Watch the cliff," he ordered.

I watched.

Never had I glued my eyes to anything the way I did to that rock precipice, scouting for *him*. A breeze puff, a plant tremble, a tiny earth slide, and I could hear the sharp intake of my breath. The mental picture of *him,* true or false, kept coming back.

I might well be accused of overactive imagination, but all sorts of things ran through my head: He was a vicious murderer escaped from Death Row at the state prison over in Arizona; he was a mental patient, considered dangerous, from the state hospital near San Diego; he was growing pot out here and simply wanted to chase us away. Maybe he was a sea gypsy? I hoped the last was true.

Aloud, my father began to count the slashes in the stern half and came up with twenty-seven. But there was plenty of fabric in the forward half that could be cut off and used to seal the holes.

At that time of day, we were very hopeful of leaving Sweet Friday. He worked away. Ten or fifteen minutes passed, then I could hear him swearing softly.

"Can I help?"

"No."

Then I asked, without looking at him, "Was Clemente trying to tell us what was out here?— *who* was out here?"

"Guess he was."

"You think he and that old woman knew someone was out here? Maybe an escaped convict?"

"He was warning us, all right, I think. Wish I'd listened. Boy, do I wish I'd listened. I've lost a boat, maybe a motor, and blown a vacation, all because I didn't listen."

"But, Daddy, why didn't he come right out and tell us, 'There's a bad man out there, don't go'?"

"I don't know. I honestly don't know." Then the soft swearing began again.

We both fell silent for a while. Finally I took my eyes off the cliff top and saw my father just sitting there on his haunches, yellow Cat cap pushed back, doing absolutely nothing, staring off to sea. He wasn't fixing the boat at all.

"I thought you said we'd get out of here before dark."

He turned his head to look directly at me, despair on his sweaty face. "We can't go."

"Why not?"

"I can't fix it, dammit. There's not enough glue." A tube was empty by his feet. "I've only patched six of these stinking holes and I've used up one whole tube." His voice was low, defeated. One more tube remained.

"What else can we do?" We had to get off that island, some way.

"I'm not sure. What I can't figure is why he slashed the boat if he wanted us off the island."

"And why did he stab my bra?"

He was still on his knees in the sand and now he shook his head, then lowered it, closing his eyes.

"Are you all right?"

"I'm a little shaky," he admitted, raising his head again. "Let's have lunch and a war council. Maybe the best thing to do is track him down and try to talk to him. You hide somewhere here, and I'll go find him."

"Don't even think about that," I said. I was convinced *he* was an escaped convict. He wouldn't think a thing of using that ax, or the gaff.

Sitting down by water's edge, we ate the rest of the deli-roasted chicken we'd had the previous night and some fruit, all the while scanning along the brink of the cliff, attempting to pierce each clump of bush. Though nothing moved up there that we could see, the threat seemed constant, hovering over the peaceful cove like an evil, unseen bird.

After a while, my father said, "There's still enough glue to fix those seats," saying it more to himself than me.

"I don't understand," I said.

He eyed me seriously. "Hang on to them and float to shore. Boca or somewhere, nearest place." The seats were about four feet long, shaped like a couch bolster when inflated. Detached from the Redshank, they could serve as floats.

For a few seconds it sounded great, then I thought about having to dangle our feet in the water. I suddenly realized that when you're caught hanging between life and death, or think you are, you hatch some pretty wild ideas. You grasp at anything to stay alive.

I asked, "What about the sharks?"

"We have to take the chance they're not man-eaters. Only a few are, ever. Honestly. Plenty of men floated around for days in World War Two and survived. Caribbean. South Pacific. Indian Ocean. It's a gamble, sure."

He went on, talking more to himself than to me. "We can grease ourselves. There's a can of it in the Mercury toolbox. That's what swimmers use. Grease."

The more I thought about it, the less I liked it. Floating thirty miles, maybe more? Our feet hanging down. It was downright scary.

My father could read my face. "You have any better ideas?"

I didn't.

He shrugged. "I can always go back to the other option—climb up there and try to find him. Reason with him."

"He took the ax," I reminded.

"Yep, he did." My father sighed.

With that, he rose up and went over to work on the life preservers, taking about an hour to fix them. With each surge, the water was rushing out of the cove, and the next rush in wouldn't come until night, not a good time to go floating on the Cortez. Just the thought of it, bobbing around in the blackness, made my heart pound.

Neither of us had mentioned this, dreading it—but night, relentlessly on its way, was now the problem. Midafternoon had arrived, and the cove would soon be in shadows. Though the realization hadn't sunk in, I suppose at that hour we were virtually prisoners of *his,* whoever *he* was, in that little half bowl, with sea ahead of us and high cliffs behind.

The damp sand was already chilling down, and I went back to the tent for my thongs, hearing my father call out, "Bring that chart and the stuff from the Hydrographic Office." He'd Xeroxed the appropriate pages on Isla Viernes Dulce and the upper Cortez rather than lug the whole fat book along.

I located them and then saw the gleaming

long butcher knife, with its honed blade, tucked in a cardboard box, along with a big barbecue fork, some smaller table knives, and our forks. I picked up the butcher knife, holding it and thinking about it, knowing that the blade was razor sharp, as always. For the first time in my life, I thought of a knife as a weapon, not a kitchen tool. Until then, the very idea of plunging a knife into someone had been too horrible to ever cross my mind. Now, I thought of it. The thought came easy.

In a moment I went back to my father's side, carrying the long knife in addition to the chart and Xeroxes.

"What's that for?" He frowned, nodding at the gleaming blade, thinking, of course, of slicing food.

"In case *he* comes down here. What else do we have, Daddy?" I guess I sounded casual.

My father looked at me strangely, shaking his head.

"Don't you want it?"

He nodded thoughtfully and said, slowly, "Yes, I guess I do." Then he frowned. "It's just that I suddenly realized he's already reduced us to thinking about a weapon, and we haven't even seen him." Disbelief was on his face. The frown deepened. "You know, Peg, I've never really thought about cutting anyone. Anyone!"

His eyes strayed up to the cliff top. I looked up, too. It was as empty as the miles of sea back to Boca de Cangrejo.

My father sighed, then said, "Thank God he didn't steal this." He reached over and ran a thumb down the sharp blade.

In a moment, he spread the chart of the upper Cortez out over the sand by the pile of Redshank. Then his fingers tapped the island area. "Now, look where Boca is, and over here south are San Felipe, Punta Estrella, Percebu, Bahia Santa Maria. . . ."

They were all places of safety, with people and roads.

He continued. "Okay, I've been thinking about sharks and dangling feet. You're right about that. So let's not take that chance. Tomorrow morning you'll float north to whichever side you can. The current begins to set west above here"—his finger tapped a spot north of the island—"but I hope a fishing boat or shrimper will pick you up long before you reach shore. Up this way are Punta San Felipe, La Ramada, Estero. . . ."

He'd said *you* twice. He hadn't said *we*.

"I'm going to strap the seats together, and you'll be safe and sound on what amounts to a pontoon. You won't need to dangle your legs in the water. Should be an easy ride, Peg, and you can send help back. There's a chopper at that airstrip in San Felipe."

"What about you?"

"Oh, I'll stay and play cat-and-mouse with him. It'll be easier to do if I know you're safe. I'll keep him occupied, believe me. I'll fix a few tricks that'll cause him some pain."

My father had to be cracking up, I thought. He wasn't thinking clearly at all. I was only fifteen but I knew better than to go out on those life cushions. I went over by them and said, "Daddy, you know a hundred times more about the sea than I do, but what happens if a wind comes up? If those seats separate, what happens? What do I do? If those patches come off, what do I do? I can swim a long way but not thirty miles. I'm sorry, I'm not going out there on those things."

He stared at me and said slowly, "You might be better off out there alone than you would in this cove if something happened to me."

He didn't need to spell that out, either—rape or death or both. But I'd made up my mind that I wasn't going anywhere on those cushions. I said, "I just won't."

He began to walk toward the overhang, saying, "You're in no position to say *won't*."

The argument was suddenly cut short when I saw some black things sailing through the air, dropping down from the cliff top toward my father. They were wriggling in slow motion, doing a sky-dive ballet, twisting and turning.

I screamed, and he looked up just as they showered down on his head and shoulders. His hands swatted frantically as he ducked and ran back toward the water. One of the things was clasped on his face, almost covering it like a black rag. He danced around.

I darted for the overhang and dived under, flattening myself against the low inner wall.

Seeing my father now in the clear, I realized what had hit him from above—spiders! A dozen or so huge spiders, with hairy legs four or five inches long. While I watched, a red-and-white Colonel Sanders chicken box came hurtling down near the Redshank pile as final insult.

About that time, I saw my father running for the crawlway, cursing loudly, butcher knife in his right hand. He'd knocked the spiders off himself and was headed up the cliff. Dirt and rock spilled down as he scrambled upward.

Barely breathing, I stayed flat against the wall, under the overhang, watching the hairy things move harmlessly back toward the cliff face. Two emerged out of the faded old Colonel Sanders box and crabbed along, headed for safety.

In a moment, my father's voice echoed down, "I can't see him."

"Don't leave me!" I yelled up, panicky that he might chase the man. I was developing a consuming fear of being left alone.

There was silence for a moment, then his reassuring voice said he was coming down.

Soon dirt slid again into the crawlway, and he appeared in front of the overhang, panting heavily. He put a supporting hand on the overhang and just stood there. His legs were trembling, I could see.

"Did they bite you?"

"I don't think so. I didn't feel it if they did. God, there was one right over my nose and mouth. Did you see that?"

"I saw it."

He ducked under and sat down beside me, blowing breath, his face crimson with exertion. "Get me a couple of sugar cubes out of the tent. I need a jolt."

When I came back, he was still panting. "You know what they were, don't you? Tarantulas! He threw down a box of tarantulas! He waited until I walked over here and then dumped them on me." He paused, staring up at the roof of the overhang. "What have we done to him?"

I shook my head. I didn't know.

He licked his lips. I noticed his face was now peach colored, the crimson slowly fading.

"You want some juice?"

He nodded.

I went back to the tent for it.

"You know what psychological warfare is, don't you?" he called out.

"Yes," I said. "He's trying to scare us."

"He's doing a damn good job. Whew! Packed in a finger-lickin' chicken box."

Then he leaned back against the wall and closed his eyes. It took a long time for the shallow, rapid breathing to ease off. He now seemed years older than he was early this morning. We sat under the overhang for fifteen or twenty minutes longer. Finally he repeated, "I wish I knew what we'd done."

There were soft murmurs of late-afternoon breeze in the brush above us—the subdued splash of the sea against the eastern shelf. There were still birdsong and sea lion bellow, but softer now. It all seemed so peaceful on Sweet Friday Island, but it was all so deadly.

CHAPTER EIGHT

Sunday Night

THE CEILING OF THE overhang was stratified in grays and browns, almost like molded concrete, with small stones embedded here and there. Since the roof sloped up gradually from the roughly three-foot height at the very back to about five feet in front, the water appeared to have eaten away at the sandstone, leaving harder rock to remain and form the overhang. This pebbly surface wasn't too different from the interior of some sea caves that I'd seen. I observed all this while sitting in that fortress, thinking I might see an awful lot of it. I didn't have much faith in floating back to the mainland, one way or another.

The overhang was, in fact, our new home away from home, our Isla Dulce Hilton vacation suite with natural air-conditioning and a lovely sea view; our prison as well.

My father was still trying to figure out what

terrible sin we'd committed this beautiful April day, and in time he estimated, "We could have invaded his little privacy. Trespassed on whatever space he's guarding. He didn't lure us here. We just barged in; didn't ask permission, didn't even say hello. We came to get privacy and stole his. Am I making sense?"

"Maybe," I said.

"Now, if he was a rational man, he would have come down here and ordered us off. But, obviously, he's not rational—throwing those tarantulas down on me. And I'm guessing he slashed our boat without thinking he'd actually strand us here. Then he looked into the tent and saw your sunglasses staring at him, accusing him, and chopped those. Don't ask me why he stole your makeup kit. He might even steal toothpicks, of course. I'm making a guess at all this. I could be totally wrong."

Or you could be totally right, I thought. My father was an amateur psychologist on occasion.

He nodded to himself. "He knows we can't leave now but doesn't know what to do about it."

"What he needs is someone to shoot him right between the eyes," I said. *Anyone who stabs a bra deserves a shot in the head,* I thought.

"Hey, hey, let's stay civilized," my father advised. "Let's try to talk to him."

"Stay civilized and talk to him? I hope you do it from two hundred feet."

"What do we have to lose?"

I again reminded him of the ax.

My father seemed to rotate back and forth between raging at the man and wanting to make peace. I could only see the man who chopped my clothes as someone very dangerous, nothing less. He should be in jail or dead, nothing in between. Nothing!

"Let me tell you a story," my father said. "A family in Pasadena was being harassed by the guy next door, yet he didn't ever outright physically threaten them. A rock on the roof in the middle of the night. Bag of garbage, one that couldn't be identified, tossed over the fence. Cat suddenly dead on the doorstep. Over months, constant things. If he'd had spiders, he'd probably have thrown 'em. These people were going out of their skulls. They were nice people who wouldn't poison his dog or wait for him some night with a baseball bat. So they sold out and left. It wasn't worth the effort. The harasser won. I'm willing to let this guy win, too. He's not worth the effort. Do you see my point, Peg?"

I didn't, really. "Why the harassment?"

"The family never knew. The man was schizophrenic, they thought. Insane but didn't appear to be. We may never know why this guy is acting up like this."

I listened to it all but still wanted the slasher dead and gone, gone, gone. Point-blank, I asked my father, nodding upward, "What do we do about tonight?"

Sweet Friday Cove was already deep in shadow. There was still some sun on the sea outside the cove, but it was becoming pale—and night was what I really feared most. Light itself was a protection, and we'd soon lose it. That tiny, damped-down fear of the dark that everyone has from babyhood on was becoming intense for me, growing into a pulsing thing. That mental picture of *him* wouldn't go away. Instead, it grew, taking form, becoming actual.

"I promise you we'll be all right," Father said, and then ducked out from under the overhang, moving quickly toward the water's edge to turn and carefully scan the cliff top. *He,* whoever he was, didn't announce himself before striking, as we now knew.

I emerged from the overhang, taking my own look over my shoulder, ready to run back. But all seemed clear.

The next thirty minutes, as I recall, were the best we'd spent since early morning. We pulled the sleeping bags from the tent and tucked them under the overhang, feet out, then gathered together the pans, clothing, fire-starter, charcoal, water, battery lantern—anything we'd need for the darkness.

My father's plan was to "hole up" for the night beneath the ledge and not come out for any reason unless *he* forced us to. We raced against the coming of night as the sun slowly pulled the light switch in the cove.

Then I heard Father say "Oops," and I asked, "What's wrong?"

"Almost forgot my sugar time."

I knew what he meant. His late-afternoon insulin injection, the diabetic blood-sugar control.

Though we'd spent a lot of father-daughter time together, both before and after the divorce, I'd never seen him give himself a shot. I didn't want to see it. I even looked away when someone was giving *me* a shot.

But I did watch now as he opened his leather medical kit, placed a new needle into the syringe, and filled it with insulin. Then I turned away as he undid his belt. The needle would go into his stomach. "No big deal," he always said.

At twilight, I dug a small fire pit that I could reach from the overhang, and we settled in for dinner. Soon flames licked cheerfully up from the charcoal briquettes. The menu was steak, potatoes, cheese, and fruit—not bad for prisoners, at that. I was always cook, because I wanted to be.

"We should have a name for that goon," my father said. "Slasher, Ripper, Knifer, Spiderman, Psycho—"

"Don't forget that he stinks."

"Stinker?"

"Why don't we just call him Señor Psycho. That's a sick, funny name." You could hear it around school.

"Fine," he said.

Then my father poured wine and made a toast: "It is time to think about all the goodness in life. Time also to toast a man I shall dub Señor Psycho, and to hope he breaks his lousy, stinking neck here tonight."

I agreed. "Here's to Psycho's broken neck."

So we had a laugh under the overhang, despite the spider man. We even had a name for him now.

"Have you imagined what he might look like?" I asked, back on that subject. I still had my own picture of him firmly fixed. My fear had photographed him.

"Not really."

"You haven't tried?"

"What good does it do?"

"I just want to take one good look at him before we leave here, from a long distance. I didn't want to see him this morning. I do now." Maybe it was the wine giving me courage.

"Oh, he might be just another sea gypsy. I told you about them, crazy *vagabundos del mar*. They sail around, then go to Isla Cerralvo to die. That's way down the gulf."

"And you don't care what Psycho looks like?" Did he have a black beard and fiery eyes? Hands the size of plates?

"No, I don't."

That's strange, I thought. *How could you not be curious?*

About that time the potatoes were done, and I grilled the steak by leaning far out from under the overhang. We soon discovered we were starved. Fear burns energy, I guess, but we hadn't eaten very much since leaving Boca.

Dinner over, my father drained the rest of the chablis into a white plastic water container and then carefully broke the half-gallon Almaden jug lengthwise, tapping out long, cruel pieces, sharp as swords on the end. They glistened in the fire glow.

I asked him what in the world he was doing.

"I'm doing some things as crazy as he does. I'm preparing a welcome. For the last two hours, off and on, while you thought I was only putting together dumb ideas, I've been conniving up in my little fertile brain. Señor Psycho is not the only clever one on this island, Peg-eye."

Maybe the wine was working on him, as well, but he seemed more at ease, more confident, more like the father I'd always known.

About eight o'clock, when there was a little more light on the cove, starshine out, a quarter moon on its way, he took the shovel over to the flat rock by the crawlway up the cliff and dug a pit about four feet deep where we'd found the bootprint. If Psycho was accustomed to stepping down there, he'd now find some falling space. I hoped he'd fall face down and bleed to death. The glass shards were carefully placed upright in the sand at the bottom of the pit. Even in the dim light, it was a fiendish-looking booby trap, twenty or so glass knives sticking up.

I didn't know my father was capable of anything like that; I'd always thought of him as a laughing, gentle, nonviolent man. Anybody who sold anything as big as earth-movers had to be gentle, I thought. "Where'd you learn that?"

"TV, I'm sure. Some jungle chase movie, I

guess. I just hope it works. For sure, he'll take some care with it, if nothing else. See, we aren't exactly helpless down here."

He came out of the pit pleased with himself and soon began emptying several cans of diet drink. We'd brought along a half dozen six-packs.

"Now what?" I asked.

"You'll see." His sly smile was shadowy.

Soon he rigged an "alarm line" about an arm's length from the ledge, just at the far end of the fire pit, using fishing line to hang the cans. They swung like gondolas. Then he dropped several pebbles into each can. They'd rattle if the line was bumped.

"TV, too?" I asked.

"Nope, original." I could tell he was grinning, and that made me feel better.

This accomplished, he took the big battery lantern for a final check of the cliff top, moving the strong beam foot by foot across the brink. Nothing moved up there, "neither hide nor hair," he said.

By nine Father was back under our rock roof, now protected by the jungle pit and the alarm system. I'd already arranged the sleeping bags side by side, even laid the butcher knife between them. It was a comforting sight, gleaming there in the firelight. Never had two souls prepared so well for the drawing night and two eyes.

He said, "I don't know what else we can do for an early-warning system. I just hope he makes a noise if he comes down here tonight."

"I'll make the noise," I assured S. J. Toland. "Your only daughter, love of your life, can have a very loud mouth at a time like this. They'll hear my scream in Boca."

"Just make sure I hear it, Dodder."

He crawled over to his tacklebox, opened it, and drew out his sharp fish-cleaning knife and whetstone; then he crawled again to where our supply of firewood was stored. He picked up a board that looked as if it were about two inches thick and four feet long, then returned to his sleeping bag.

"Now what are you going to do?" I asked.

"You'll see in the morning."

I could easily wait. I was totally bushed, and I slipped down into my bag. This day had seemed without end. Father stayed on top of his bag, resting his back against the cliff wall, carving away at the board in the lantern light. I had a thought that the carving might be for show, that he was really playing watchman.

A few minutes later, a sound came down from

the cliff top and curled into the overhang, a drawn-out cry that was more animal than human. I'd heard coyotes howl in the desert, and this sound was almost the same.

My father switched off the lantern and reached for the butcher knife. "That's no coyote!" He knew animal cries.

"It's *him!*" I began to shake.

"Probably. Don't let it get to you."

"Why doesn't God just kill him?" I whispered. *Strike him dead.*

"God doesn't kill," my father said. "God heals."

The howl sound went on and on, seeming to flow into our hideaway, inhuman and chilling.

My father's free hand came over to grasp mine. He said calmly, trying to reassure me, "I told you about harassing today, didn't I? That's what he's doing, Peg. Giving us a little prebedtime treatment. He knows we're under here. Let him howl his fool head off. He'd probably like me to come out and shine the light. I won't do it."

I couldn't speak. *I could not even speak.*

He howled again.

Then everything went quiet.

"Has he gone?" I asked, hearing my own voice quiver. "Psycho" was no longer a funny name. Just sick. That earlier picture I had of him—a thick-necked, big-bellied white man with long black hair and cold eyes and huge hands and a wet mouth—came rushing back.

"I don't know, but I think he realizes I won't take the bait and come out. If he wants us, he has to come down here and get us."

I ached to go to sleep, just wanting to fade out completely. I fought it for what seemed a long while but wasn't at all. Then I heard my father say, "I think he's gone, Peg." Even though I was already flat, I felt like collapsing.

Soon I heard a brittle laugh. "Well, your mother will say, 'Aha, I told you so. Your father's a fool. You both could have been killed.' And, you know, she'll be right."

I answered the only way I could. "I love you, and I know you didn't mean this to happen."

He was silent.

"Say something with me, will you, Daddy?"

"Sure."

"Now I lay me down to sleep,
I pray the Lord my soul to keep.
When I awake and see the light,
'Tis God who kept me through the night."

There was a pause, and then he whispered, "I haven't said that with you in a long, long time."

Please, God, keep us.

I wished my father a good night, and he murmured the same to me.

For a little longer, I strained to hear any sound at all. There was only the perpetual soft, wet lap in the cove and the heavier pound of the small breakers along the east side of the island. The low drum carried through the strata of rock, and that's the last I heard.

CHAPTER NINE
Monday Morning

WHEN I SLOWLY AWAKENED, it was well past
dawn, and I stayed still and prone a few minutes,
just looking seaward. The morning was fresh and
beautiful outside the cove—sea glittering again,
sky cobalt blue and cloudless. It was as if yesterday,
that awful endless day, had been something
dreamed or imagined, nothing real. Señor Psycho
didn't exist!

Then I looked over at my father. He seemed
smaller than usual.

Bundled in his navy jacket, yellow-capped
head sagging, whiskery chin on his chest, he was
still on top of his sleeping bag, left hand on a
wooden rifle, of all things, right hand loosely on the
fish knife. Wood chips were all over his legs and
the sand around him. There was still a weak peep
of light coming from the battery lantern.

A wooden gun.

I was amazed. He'd probably carved most of the night away. If it had been painted black, or dark gray, the rifle, from a distance, would have looked absolutely real. The barrel appeared to be made of a piece of black rubber tubing, maybe off the outboard. He'd even put a trigger and trigger guard on it, likely swiped from some part of the Mercury. He'd been busy, all right. Never underestimate an engineering major from Cal Tech.

In fact, Psycho might stop playing his dirty games if he saw us with a gun. I immediately felt better. This day would be a good one, I thought. We were fighting back.

I leaned closer, saying, "We made it, Daddy," shaking him gently.

He awakened with a start, stared at me wide eyed, then relaxed.

"We're okay," I said.

"I'm glad," he murmured tiredly, closing his eyes again.

"That's a good-looking gun. I wish it would shoot."

He laughed softly and began gathering his senses. "Hey, what about this gun. Sweet Friday Winchester. This is a piece of old, ordinary Douglas fir, two by six. I didn't know I could carve,

Peg. Not bad, eh? Now I've got to figure out a way to stain it."

"You carved all night?"

"Most of it. Psycho didn't come back, that I know of."

The charcoal briquettes in the fire pit were powder gray, and the alarm system hung forlornly outside the overhang, untried, dew dripping from the pebbled cans. Unfortunately, *he* wasn't impaled in the glass dagger pit by the crawlway, a gory mess, mouth open, cold eyes fixed, deader 'n ashes.

My father looked all around. "And isn't this a kick? Seven-Up can alarm system, jungle pit, and phony rifle. Remind me to take pictures today. No one is going to believe how that Redshank looks unless I photograph it. My insurance man sure as shootin' won't."

He glanced down at the gun. "And I'm real proud of this. That's not a bad stock. Needs some sandpaper, that's all. I think if I grind up some charcoal, mix it with motor oil, it'll look pretty authentic."

Yes, it would. "You never got into that sleeping bag. Aren't you cold?"

"A little. Time to get the blood pumping." He got stiffly to his knees, scraping off the chips. "Stay here while I check."

He put the rifle down and crawled on out, then stood and went to the center of the beach, scanning all along the cliff top.

"Looks safe," he said, proceeding on over to the johnny area behind the big rock on the far right side of the cove. A few minutes later he emerged and went down to the surf line to splash water on his face, prior to rinsing with a little fresh water from one of the white plastic jugs. We always conserved that way, even when brushing teeth.

Still secure and snug in my sleeping bag, I watched him, thinking that the day was starting off well.

My father was still standing by the surf line, his back to the cliff, when there was a rumble, then a tremendous thud above me on the overhang. I saw a boulder about three feet in diameter bounce high, become airborne, and then roll toward him. He turned and spotted it, but the massive rock had already been slowed by the sand, and he wasn't in any danger.

Sprinting back toward me, he grabbed the long knife off the sleeping bag and headed for the crawlway, yesterday's fury back on his face. He looked almost like a wild animal, leaping over the sand pit and starting to climb, yellow cap falling into the pit.

Afraid of what might happen up there, but just as scared of staying under the ledge without him, I scrambled out of the sleeping bag, tugged on my shoes, rounded the overhang, jumped across the pit, and headed up the crawlway. I was beginning to do things automatically, reacting without really thinking.

Feet pushing up, my fingers dug into the dirt. Unless you are standing directly beneath it, a forty- or fifty-foot vertical doesn't seem to be a great height. But climbing it, midway up, you feel as if you're hanging from the side of a high rise. Looking down at the beach only once, a mistake, I forced myself on up and finally got to the top, throwing my body over the edge, rolling and calling out for my father.

He was there, all right, standing on that tranquil plateau, holding the butcher knife, hair all messed up, shirttail hanging out. He was beginning to look as wild as the man he was chasing.

"You see him?" I asked.

"Not a trace."

We both looked up-island over the rocks and brush, most of it knee to waist high. Nothing moved.

There was a serene feeling of early-morning desert up there, with the sun thinly golden rather than white hot. We'd felt that serenity and seen that southwest light before. A gentle, cool breeze flowed over us.

"I thought I might spot him," said my father, knife in hand.

Oddly enough, I felt momentary relief that he hadn't. Climbing up, I'd had visions of my father locked in a fight with *him*. *Oh, if we could just get off, let Psycho have his stinking, rotten, forsaken island, and all the privacy he ever wanted.*

"He's really getting comic, Peg. Pushing boulders down, for Lord's sake. You know what? I'm less afraid of him today. This kind of nonsense makes me less afraid. But it's still for real."

"You were afraid of him yesterday?"

My father blinked. "Why, yes. Yes, I was terribly afraid of him. I looked at that ruptured boat and I was afraid, for both of us."

I said, "Well, I felt better today when I woke up."

"That's the ticket."

The boulder hadn't landed within forty feet of my father, but it was the threat of it, I'm sure—what it did to us mentally. Whatever *his* intent, the idea of being mashed was enough to push all sorts of mental buttons.

"He's got others lined up like bowling balls out there, the fiendish SOB," my father said, pointing to the cliff edge. "He must have done it last night before he began that phony howling. I think what he wanted me to do was step out from under the overhang, then he'd mash me. What about that?"

Four more boulders, all at least three feet in diameter, were poised on the brink. "I know something about weight and mass. These must weigh upward of a ton each," my father said. "If one hit you, you'd be just a dark stain."

I didn't want to look at them any longer.

I took a long look around up there. As might be expected, the view of the island was entirely different from that of the sea surface and not exactly consoling. We were standing on a starved hog's back, about where the head and shoulders might be. To the north, land ridged up on both sides like ribs, rising to the backbone, which humped up to the high point—the 306 feet the navy described—about three-quarters of the way along. Gorges and ravines, some little more than gullies or washes, appeared to slice down the central ridge. As it neared the sea on each side of the half-mile width, the land sheared away to the bird-limed cliffs. As far as I could see, there wasn't a single bush more than three or four feet high on the entire top of Isla Viernes Dulce. Most of the pale green was from cactus, poking out here and there against the bronze, metallic earth—the brown-gray-black of rock.

Though the breeze wasn't at all chilly, I shivered, the same way I'd done in the bucking Toyota on Saturday. Again, it was a mental shiver more than a physical one.

Even sun-splashed, the land before me was so bleak, so rugged, that I wondered how *he* could exist out here—*why* he'd want to. He was alone, I guessed. I knew there were loners who lived in the wilderness and loved it. I knew that hermits even lived in big cities. Strange people lived in strange places, I knew, and likely most of them weren't dangerous. But I had an idea that this one, a man who knifed bras, tossed tarantulas, and shoved boulders, was *very* dangerous. I kept my thoughts to myself.

Whoever he was, whatever he was, we'd made a terrible mistake in wanting to come to this "irresistible island," and the contrast between the beautiful cove below us and the top of Sweet Friday was astonishing.

I could see both the east shore of Baja and, to my right, the mainland side, Mexico proper. Sharp against the morning sun, Cerro Piñacato rose up from over there. The sight of both shores, so near, yet so far away, was cruel and punishing.

My father broke up my reverie. "Come here, Peg."

I walked over.

The dirt had been disturbed for six or seven yards behind the cliff brink where the boulders had been rolled to the edge. "Look here," said my father. "He used something to pry the rocks last night, a fulcrum of some kind, but all of this is old back here. He didn't plan this yesterday or last night. He's been preparing for visitors for a long time. See, the wind has blown dust over his old tracks; rain has washed them. He might have pushed some of them along the top of the island for a quarter mile. You know what he has here—an arsenal, a damned rock arsenal."

Footprints were everywhere, the same insolent heavy boots we'd seen by the crawlway. My flesh tingled looking down at them, my mind again building *him* up from his big feet.

We went over to the boulders, where the bootprints were fresh from last night. "Look, he's chocked them on the beach side with small rocks. All he has to do is tap the rocks out, put his shoulder here, and over they'll go. Here, I'll show you."

My father kicked the chocks out from one, then pushed the boulder. It rumbled down the cliff face, hit the overhang, bounced high, and rolled briefly down the sand. He shook his head in disbelief. "He placed them here so he could actually bomb the beach. Peg, you know this is what cavemen used to do. This is how they tried to stun dinosaurs. Now do you get a better picture of this guy's weedy brain?"

Not one that I liked to think about.

We unchocked the other three rocks and shoved them. Down they went over the cliff, like tanks, crashing on the overhang and bouncing, a ton of rock each. They sat like sentinels on the beach, not too far from the Redshank's remains.

Just as the last one hit the ledge and bounced, I thought I heard a far-off engine drone. "You hear that? Outboard, I think."

My father shook his head and began to look up-island for Psycho again, single-minded.

I ran to the east side of the mesa and soon spotted two specks on the horizon in the direction of Boca de Cangrejo. Tiny white arrows on the water, they moved steadily south and would pass us, far out. I yelled, "Boats!" and Father ran over.

"They're probably the ones we saw up on the beach at Boca. Fishermen."

"They'll never hear us," I said.

"But, hell's bells, maybe they can see us. You bring a mirror? Scramble down for it."

"I had a metal one. That old one I always bring."

"Had?" he exploded.

"The makeup bag, remember?"

"Okay, get anything that will shine. Bean can, anything. Hurry."

He called after me, "Get the binoculars, too."

I went banging down the cliff on my buns, barely feeling the rough earth and sharp rocks. It was the first break we'd had since landing in the cove, and I would have skidded down naked, frontside to the dirt, if it would have helped.

A moment later, I was clawing back up, one handed, glasses slung around my neck. The other hand held a tin tomato can. I just dug in and went up, fingernails long broken, anyway.

Up on the plateau, I raced for my father, rubbing the bottom of the can on my shirt front. I could still hear the far-off boats' buzz, two separate and distinct outboard whines.

He grabbed the can excitedly, saying, "Sun's in the right position," and began sending an SOS in Morse code, which he knew from his navy days in World War II. The hot stabs of light went out from the top of Sweet Friday again and again. *Three dots, three dashes, three dots.*

He kept sending long after we'd lost sight of

the skiffs, after the engine whines had faded out. We couldn't help but feel some despair, yet we knew we could signal again.

He angled the can toward Boca and sent for five or ten minutes. Maybe Raul Clemente or someone outside the cantina would spot the flashes and understand them.

I adjusted the powerful Zeiss binoculars and could actually see the little village. Through the magnified lenses, it looked so close. Maybe we could float safely to it, after all.

I heard my father saying "They'll spot us sooner or later. We'll do this every time a boat passes." He sounded hopeful, but as I took the glasses down from my eyes, his face wasn't all that optimistic.

"We can try again this afternoon when they return to Boca, can't we?" I asked.

"Not until morning. The sun will be in the wrong place this afternoon. But if something passes on the other side, we'll give 'em a flying fit, Peg-eye."

"You bet," I said, trying to sound encouraging myself. "You want to look at Boca?"

I passed over the glasses.

He took his own look and then grumped, "This'll drive you nuts, looking over there. Looks like it's two miles away."

"Wonder if the Land Cruiser's okay."

"Sure it is," he said.

"Clemente still thinks we're on Isla Piño, doesn't he?"

"That's what my note said. I can't change it now. That's what I get for being tricky and lying."

"I'm ready to try and float over there," I announced.

"Let's hold that for very last. I think you're absolutely right about dangling legs for shark bait. Another bad idea of mine. Now I've got to pump some insulin into my gut, and then let's have some breakfast. You still cook that super bacon? I can smell it now." He put on a bright smile.

"Then do what?" *What, dear Father, are our plans for this sunny day?*

"Track down our funny host."

"And?"

The smile faded like those outboard sounds. "I don't know."

We made a slow, thoughtful trip back down the cliff face.

CHAPTER TEN

Midmorning

AFTER WE ATE, I spent most of a half hour polishing the bottom of a saucepan, scouring it in the damp sand, then applying Brillo until it gleamed. My father figured we needed more signaling reflection surface than the tomato can provided. Meanwhile, he ground up several charcoal briquettes and mixed them with motor oil, coming up with a color that wasn't black but was dark enough to fool Psycho, we hoped. He rubbed it into the phony gun and then walked to the far side of the cove, posing with it like an Old West sheriff.

"How does this look?" He aimed it toward the Redshank.

From seventy-five feet, or abouts, absolutely real. "Load it," I said. Oh, how I wished for that! I took a photo of him.

Then he came back to the overhang and made

a belt sheath for the butcher knife. The blade stuck down about fifteen inches, like a sword. After that, he snipped off about thirty feet of line from the boat anchor, saying we might need it up there. He coiled it neatly, to slip over his shoulder. Above all, we wanted our hands free.

I went about packing big navel oranges, bread, and Monterey Jack cheese into a small canvas bag (relic from Toland days of wooden tent stakes) and then filled a much-used army canteen with fresh water. The top of the island would be fiercely hot by midmorning, we knew.

All of this was preparation for war on Sweet Friday, demented as it might be. At first, my father thought I should stay behind and hide—safer that way—but changed his mind after I made a big fuss. Only if the U.S. Marines had been around would I have stayed alone in that cove.

Finally, at about eleven that bright Monday morning, the make-do father-daughter Toland reconnaissance and expeditionary force got under way on Isla Viernes Dulce. At best, we were an odd-looking combat outfit.

I took a picture of my father wearing a T-shirt that advertised Hussong's, a famous bar in Ensenada, a town on the west coast of Baja. The butcher knife was strapped on one side, the canteen on the other, rope and binoculars were slung around his neck, the yellow cap planted on his head. He carried the charcoaled wooden rifle "at the ready" and seemed to be trying to look tough. At least, he wasn't smiling. Just from appearance, he posed no threat to anyone that day.

Nor did I. I heaved myself up the cliff ahead of him. The gravel got worse each time, and my hands were already scratched all over.

On top we saw that nothing had changed in the last three hours, except for the invasion of a busy bunch of dragonflies. They were helicopter-ing all over the place. Up the line, perched and squabbling sea birds could be heard. From below, sea lions were adding their coughing say-so.

But there was no howling, murderous com-mittee of one to greet us, and the jagged, burned landscape to the north, with the fuzzy chollas and ocotillos sticking out here and there, remained still, caught in the deep desert quiet. The brilliant Baja sun, almost overhead now, had routed shad-ows from the gullies that were immediately in front of us. The troughs went down to the guano facings, probably spillways for the brief, hard win-ter rains of the Cortez.

Father said, "Let's go along the side here, then try to get up on the ridge. Maybe we can look down on him." There was a worn pathway there.

So we started out, scattering the birds ahead

as we walked, hugging the east side of the island, about fifteen or twenty feet from the drop-off to the sea. The tide was already vacating the shelf down there. In a short time we could retreat to the shelf and move along it, if necessary.

Earlier my father had said it made sense that there'd be some kind of hut or shelter somewhere near the spring. The Hydrographic Office claimed the spring existed somewhere on the north end. Hauling water the shortest distance possible should always dictate where you stay in the wilderness, especially the desert. That was a basic I'd been taught long ago.

He said, "If we can locate *his* camp from above, then we might be able to figure out a safe approach down and talk to the idiot, tell him all we want to do is leave here."

I was all for that. Quickly. Today. Just get off and go home.

Where *he* was at that very moment, exactly what he was doing, gnawed at me as we walked along, low brush clutching at our legs. Was he watching from the ridge top, making his own plans? Did he see that my father was carrying a rifle? Had he circled around behind us to stalk?

We both looked back every so often. Though I fought it, there was that constant tap of fear in my stomach, and I think it was tapping in Sam

Toland's belly, too. It was certainly on his mind.

"We can spot him in plenty of time if he comes rushing down off that ridge. We have running room along here."

Something had bothered me since yesterday. "Do you think he has a gun?"

"I don't think so. He would have taken a potshot at us long before now, just to scare us."

All the same, I think my father, too, had worried about hearing a sharp crack in the air—the whine of a bullet.

We'd gone several hundred yards when the first panic button was pushed. I saw motion about 60 feet inland, a mushroom of dust, and I frantically grabbed the back of the Hussong shirt. Unable to speak, I pointed. The browns and bronzes made everything difficult to spot, but something was definitely moving over there.

He focused the binoculars and finally murmured, "Iguana," passing the glasses over.

A big one, the harmless lizard was moving sluggishly up toward the ridge, stirring dust.

We went on like a pair of lost privates in a minefield, careful where we stepped, twice pressing corrugated soles into scorpions, once gladly yielding to a tarantula on the trail—up close, they come near to being hideous. Snakes were another matter. We kept scanning the rough ground ahead for them. Now and then, we heard rustlings, but no rattles.

Moving through the sparse knee-high brush and cactus, then over the rust-red gravel, dipping into shallow gullies, but once scrambling in and out of a ravine about eight feet deep—scouring it for creepy-crawlies before going down—it took nearly fifteen minutes to reach a spot opposite the high point of the ridge—the 306 feet above sea level.

There we rested while my father raked the whole crestline with the binoculars. Carved against the noon sky, the partial saddleback was empty of humanity.

Finally, he said, "Okay, Dodder, let's go up and see where the SOB lives. Pardon the profanity."

"Pardoned," I said.

The land rose at about thirty degrees, deceptively rougher than it looked, and half the time we were on hands and knees, getting toeholds then grinding up. I fell once, sliding back about 10 feet, skinning my elbows and ripping my shirt. My father came back to help, but I was already up and moving, hands and elbows bleeding and stinging.

Sweaty and puffing, we reached the summit. Making me stay back a few feet, my father very cautiously poked his head over the crown and said, "Well, what do you know, Señor Psycho does have himself a camp."

"Do you see him?"

"No," he replied, easing back down to where I was after a few minutes of observation. Uncertainty was in his eyes.

We rested, had some water, ate some cheese and bread and two of the oranges, leaving enough for a later snack for my father. Then we crawled back to the edge to use the binoculars. "You think he knows we're here?" I asked.

He craned his head around, taking off the yellow cap to wipe sweat from the band. "That question'll get us a ride on the next ferryboat to Boca. Who knows what he knows or doesn't know? What he thinks or doesn't think? He's bonkers and is liable to be anywhere, do anything. You've seen that already." He handed me the glasses for my own look.

I focused in sharp. *His* half shelter was in a kind of pocket, with a natural low rock wall behind it. The camp was on a little mesa at the very northwest corner of the island, a rectangle of rock and dirt. The west and north sides appeared to drop into the sea. I saw no boats anywhere, at least none that he'd hauled out for us to conveniently steal.

From this distance, it was difficult to make out detail—but the shelter had a lean-to roof on it, and the sides appeared to be made of weathered, unpainted boards. There was a dropcloth over the front, probably canvas, and something was waving in the air near it. That turned out to be a shirt on a laundry line. I gave the glasses back.

My father changed the calibration and peered awhile longer. "It's no palace, is it?"

"Where do you think he is right now?"

My father sighed. "I can't answer that."

"I wish you'd try," I said, unable to shed myself of that mental picture of a very big man with big hands.

"Let's hope we'll flush him out."

"Are you ready?" I asked. If we kept delaying going down to that hut, I'd lose what little courage I'd worked up.

"Where do springs grow?" Exasperatingly, he kept on examining the camp and jabbering.

"How should I know?" I snapped.

Two people in this kind of situation soon begin to zap each other. Even fathers and daughters. After a while, you feel like you're exploding. The mesa heat didn't help.

He answered his own question. "Where there is fresh water and enough pressure to push it up."

Oozing sweat, I was really getting jumpy up

there. But he went blithely on, "He's got a nice, safe layout. Probably unapproachable from the sea where his hut is. He's got that sheltering cliff partly to the north; the ridge is to the east. South is open, and that's where he may be taking his walks toward us. One thing, if you look at that hut, he's been around for a while. Maybe he is a *vagabundo*."

I just wanted my father to shut his mouth and start moving. Maybe he was doing all that talking because he didn't want to go down that slope. I said, "Daddy, please, let's go."

"I'll tell you something else," he said, ignoring my request. "Walking into that camp from the north over that little cliff doesn't do much for me. Coming up from the south doesn't, either. I think I'll just go down over this ridge to say hi to him. Okay?"

I repeated, "Please, let's go. I think I may throw up." I was beginning to feel that way.

He turned. "You're not going, Peg. You're staying up here, out of trouble."

I shook my head. "Daddy, you're not leaving me alone anywhere on this island. I swear that. I told you that. I'll follow you no matter where you go."

He stared at me for a moment. "Okay, let's do it. Just stay back of me, and if he comes toward us, you *run*. You damn well run like hell. Understand me, Peggy?"

"Yes, I understand you."

Soon we were scuffling our way along the ridge like mountain goats, just beneath the crown, trying to keep from sliding downward. Only our heavy breathing and the slither of dirt and gravel interrupted the high-noon siesta of ancient Isla Viernes Dulce.

Every so often Father checked our progress, trying to determine when we'd be opposite the lean-to. As happened, it took about twenty minutes of grunting and stiff-legged clinging until we were above the schizoid's little dirt patch by the sea. We sank down, rested, and had some more water.

A few minutes later, my father crawled to the crown on his belly to peer down through the binoculars.

"See him?"

"Nope."

"See the spring?"

"It must be tucked away underneath, hidden by the slope. Maybe right below us."

I crawled up beside him, and he handed the glasses over. "He might be inside the lean-to."

Nothing moved down in that camp except the blue shirt on the laundry line.

My father said, "Okay, Peg, let's do it. Leave that stupid pot and the glasses up here. We'll get 'em on the way back."

I was only too happy to leave the saucepan. It had been banging my tailbone ever since I'd shifted it around to my back.

Holding the rifle as if it were real, he sighed. "Wish John Wayne was here." My father could usually say something to break tension.

But I didn't feel it breaking this day.

CHAPTER ELEVEN

Monday Afternoon

WE STARTED DOWN, slipping and sliding more than walking, sending down rivulets of loose dirt. I tried to keep my eyes on the camp below but had to keep glancing down at the slope for footing. About thirty feet from the bottom, after we'd gone over a little hump, the spring came into view. Deep in the rectangle, it was little more than a crevice.

My father stopped at that point to look around again, holding the rifle prominently, showing it off, hoping that Psycho would be fooled by it and not rush us. We didn't consider it would have the exact reverse effect and keep him hidden. We wanted to see him.

"Anyone here? Anyone home?" The shouted words broke the hush of the mesa.

There was no answer.

In the area of the spring, the slope skidded

down steeply, a sheer of seven or eight feet; but off to the right was a place to inch down, and we veered that way.

Standing by the spring, my father yelled again, "Hello! Anyone there?"

Silence!

We were still a hundred feet from the wood-and-tin lean-to, and after the shout the silence rushed back in ominously. The afternoon Cortez breeze was picking up and crooning over us, creating little dust devils.

"Mister, are you there? Señor, are you there? ¿Comprende? We mean no harm. Peace, man. Paz! PEACE! Understand peace?"

No shaggy head poked out of the hut.

"Hey, hey, hey, hey, hey!" shouted my father.

The words echoed across the plateau and slid uselessly into the sea.

"Señor, por favor! Habla!"

Nothing.

"Hey, do you speak English?"

My father yelled on for a few minutes and then gave up, kneeling down by the spring. He dipped a finger into the milky water and tasted it. "Lot of alkali."

But I cupped some in my hands and generously washed my face. I was feeling dust in every pore. The smelly water felt tremendous.

He said, "Okay, let's go on over. Stay behind me. Right behind me."

We went to within fifty feet of the hut and stopped again.

"If he won't talk from here, he won't talk at all," said my father. He shouted again at the tin and boards.

The half cover on the front, from that distance, turned out to be a canvas tarpaulin. We couldn't see inside, as the tarp extended almost to the ground.

My father took the long knife out of the sheath and held it alongside the gun. "Stay here. I'm going on up. Keep looking around and yell if you see him coming."

"Please be careful," I said.

He just grunted and kept walking, like John Wayne would, very, very slowly.

I looked side to side, every direction, just in case *he* came running out.

Finally I saw my father use the rifle barrel to gently move the tarp aside. "No one's here," he said.

John Wayne had done his job, thank God.

Then I realized how jelly-weak my knees were, but I wobbled on them up to him anyway.

There wasn't any bedding on the swept earth floor. No cooking gear. No clothes. It appeared *he*'d abandoned the hut, knowing we'd discover it. But he had lived there, for certain, and for a long time. A Mexican furniture-store calendar, a nude sprawled on it, was tacked up on one side.

My father said, "Looking at this, I can't get any estimate on him, can you? Big, little, young, old . . ."

"Where'd he go?" I asked.

"Where's the ax?" he asked.

No red handle was visible in or around the hut. No gaff, either.

"But I can sure smell him here," I said. "It's that same body smell that was in the tent."

My father turned and suddenly shouted, "Where the hell are you?"

Only that unforgettable Isla Viernes Dulce silence answered. More than ever, I wanted to be home, safe in that cul-de-sac on Crescent Way; wanted to be where there were lights and cars and people. Even smog.

To the side of the hut, in shade, was a fire ring, and my father went over there, putting a hand down on the rocks. "Ouch! Still hot. He cooked here this morning!"

We circled to the back of the hut. Some wood was stacked. No ax.

"Do you think he might have a boat that's hidden?"

"Maybe." He was already walking toward the south end of the mesa, and I ran to catch up.

Psycho's footprints seemed to have been swept away; there was no sign of tracks leading from the mesa in any direction. And then we came to a dead stop because there was a ravine at least twenty feet deep and about eight feet wide on the south end of the rectangle. There was no way for my father or me to jump it.

He was looking down into that sliced earth and its prickly tangle, a big frown on his forehead. He said slowly, worriedly, "He must be able to walk on air when he wants to."

The ravine stretched back to the steep slope, and the other way, too, west, over to the sea. My father went on, "And I'll tell you something else. I'll bet you ten to one that he's now holed up in one of those caves, and I'll bet twenty to one that they're on up past this ravine."

The Hydrographic Office had mentioned the caves, I remembered.

"Why would he want to stay in a cave?"

"I haven't the slightest—"

He looked both ways again and then sighed. "We'll come back in the morning."

"You don't want to try and find him now?"

"Let's go. I've had it for today." The diabetes was probably taking its toll.

It's early afternoon. We could try to climb in and out of that ravine, I thought, *go down this side of the island—look for other paths, look for him. Find the caves, at least.*

"You don't want to find him?" I asked.

My father stared back at me.

We stood there looking at each other for a moment. I think he knew what I was thinking— that he was avoiding this man, that he'd lost his courage. As much as I didn't want it to happen, my hero, my ten-foot-tall father, began to shrink.

Then I said something that I regretted immediately. "Are you still afraid of him, Daddy?"

He blinked, swallowed, and answered, "I've already told you I'm scared to death of him."

I felt my world tilt further out from under me.

He kept looking at me and then added quietly, "But I'll kill him if I have to."

Whenever I'd said *kill,* it was always a physically harmless word. "I could *kill* Stevie for telling my mother . . ." But I'll never forget the way my father said it that day. So quietly, so tiredly, so desperately.

I knew he meant it.

CHAPTER TWELVE
Midafternoon

TALKING HARDLY AT ALL, we climbed back to the ridgeline and settled in the hot dirt to watch the camp through the binoculars, hoping Señor Psycho might come out of his mesa after we'd gone. After a fruitless half hour of that, my father shined the bottom of the saucepan on his pants, wiping off the dust, and began to flash SOS toward the west and San Felipe. We could see Mexican shrimpers, out of San Felipe, chugging along in the distance.

After fifteen or so minutes of that, he gave up, and we went down the slope to the east side of the guano cliffs and walked slowly back toward the cove in strained silence. It had not been a good day.

My father, being an outdoorsman, was more agile than most men his age, but even that luck ran out when we were renavigating that eight-foot gully about midway to the cove. I was already up and easily out of it when he lost his footing and skidded back down the dirt V, landing with his left ankle bent under, dropping the wooden gun, yelling out in pain.

I saw him sitting down there and asked if he was okay. He looked up, face contorted. He was holding his left ankle, cap askew. He looked pathetic.

"Want me to come down?"

He shook his head and finally stood. "I might have sprained it."

He pulled himself up to the edge of the crevice, then I helped him on up. In a moment he was hobbling for the cliff edge, leaning on me.

"I would have to ding my foot, not my dumb head," he complained.

Diabetics always fear foot injuries because of poor blood circulation. Suddenly I was angry at him for falling, for being awkward, for laming himself at a time like this.

The going was slow, and it took almost a half hour to reach the cove. We stopped once to rest, and he popped a couple of sugar cubes into his mouth.

Before we started to scale down, we took a long look over the edge, just in case. But the blue dome tent was still up, the flattened Redshank hadn't been disturbed, and the sand pit with its shining glass needles, direct from jungle movies on the late-late show, was still vacant, waiting patiently in the afternoon sun for the maniac.

Yet we immediately knew he'd visited again in our absence. New footprints were around. Those hard, plain cowboy boot heels had been all over the sand near the tent and overhang.

My father said simply, "You can't be two places at once."

Scaling down the crawlway to the cove was difficult for him. He decided to go down on his backside so that he wouldn't put any weight on his left foot. So he held it up in the air and braked himself with his right foot. I helped him over the sand pit, and then he sat down, breathing heavily.

I said, "I'll inspect."

He nodded.

Something odd was happening out on Isla Viernes Dulce—over and beyond the madman's harassment. We were beginning to take things in stride, not make a big thing out of what he was doing, no matter what he did. Perhaps it was because we were exhausted and didn't know it. Perhaps it was because it was like being in a game—when it starts you're anxious and nervous and sometimes frightened. Then it settles down, and you begin to play to win. This time, maybe to kill.

Walking to the overhang, because his footprints led there, I bent under and gasped. The blue thermos of fresh water was on its side, cap lying in damp sand nearby. It had been half-full. I glanced at the soldierly row of our white plastic supermart jugs containing fresh water. Damp sand again. I crawled in to take a closer look. Psycho had punctured all but one of the jugs, somehow missing it. So we had enough fresh water for a day or two, if we limited it to drinking and used it sparingly.

I told my father that our fresh water was mostly gone.

He answered tonelessly, "I guess he's trying to force us to drink from his lousy spring, make the trip there." Then a moment later, he asked, "You move our fishing rods?" They'd been leaning up against the overhang, near the outboard.

"Nope." I looked over.

"Well, he's not content to fool with the water. He wants to cut the food supply, too."

Still on my knees in the sand, I noticed the sleeping bags. A flash of deep red came from my father's bag. I crawled over there. Something bloodlike had been smeared around the neck of it. A knife had been doing a little more slashing. I looked over at my own bag, which appeared untouched.

I said to my father, "Now, he went after your sleeping bag." I sniffed the red stuff. "Catsup, I think."

Over by the tent, I could see that the Heinz bottle had been half emptied and was on its side in the sand.

I returned to my father's side, asking what I could do.

He replied, "Really a great time to sprain my ankle, but that's what I think I've done. No breaks that I can feel. See, it's starting to swell. Get me a towel and some ice. I'll try to knock down the swelling."

There was ice in both coolers, over which he always kept a blanket to slow down melting. I decided to draw the ice out of the one in which we stored a few diet drinks, orange juice, butter, cheese, and other food. So I only opened one of the boxes and soon had an ice pack ready.

Meantime, my father crawled to the overhang and ducked under. He began the ice treatment on the ankle, which was turning blue around the knobby bone. I had the feeling that my father wasn't going to do very much walking on Sweet Friday Island for several days.

First things first. I scraped the gunk out of his sleeping bag, wiped the bag down with a moistened cloth, and then draped it over one of the big "bombing rocks" that were now down on the sand. The sun was departing the cove, but there was a little breeze leaking in from the south and it would help a bit to dry the lining.

While I went about getting ready for the night, I kept thinking that the best thing to do, now that my father could no longer walk, was for me to spend the entire day tomorrow up on the cliff's edge, flashing that pan at Boca de Cangrejo in the morning, at San Felipe in the afternoon. Some fishing or shrimping boat might see it if the people on shore couldn't. If the maniac came along, I'd just scoot down the crawlway to safety.

I was just about to tell my father about that plan when I went over to the other cooler box for a frozen container of beef stroganoff that he'd made the week before. There were a half dozen containers of various prepared foods in the cooler. Also always stored in there on these trips was the large leather shaving kit, wrapped in a plastic bag, that contained his insulin supply, needles, syringes, and other things he needed to treat himself medically.

Knowing he'd taken his morning shot, I

looked over at him. "Where'd you put the kit? I can't see it in here."

He knocked the towel-wrapped ice into the sand, moving on his hands and knees over to me. Bending over the cooler, pushing food around frantically, he said, "I had it this morning."

I knew that.

Panic was in his voice as he said, "Maybe I put it back in the other cooler."

But I already knew it wasn't there, either, before he ripped open the latch and looked inside. Only the diet six-packs and the half-gallon jugs of orange juice were visible.

Suddenly there was an anguished moan from his lips, not even words, and he went back on his haunches, closing his eyes. I had not seen my father cry since the divorce, and then he had only broken down once, on Christmas Eve. Now as he sat on his haunches in the sand of the quiet cave, tears rolled down his cheeks, though he fought them back. His whole body shook. It was awful to see. That's another Sweet Friday Island scene, heart and gut wrenching, that I'll remember until I die. His tears tore at me.

In a moment, he regained control of himself and murmured apologetically, "Sorry, Peg-eye, but I just get such a feeling of helplessness with this miserable disease." Then he lifted his reddened eyes up to where the cliff edge was and said, "God damn him, God damn him," and it wasn't the least bit profane.

What else could I do but agree?

Dragging the injured ankle, he crawled back to where he'd been sitting, rescued the ice pack out of the sand, asked for another towel, and began treating the ankle again. "Now we'll have to figure some things out. There's not too much time."

Within a day or two, or less, he could slip into a diabetic coma. From that state, he would slip into death.

CHAPTER THIRTEEN

Monday Night

"WHY HE TOOK THAT shaving kit, I have no idea—and maybe he had none, either, like why he took your makeup bag—but I want you to promise you won't try to get anything back, no matter what. Just let him take what he wants; fishing rods, the shaving kit, the tent, the outboard motor, whatever the SOB wants. Promise."

"Just let him take what he wants," I repeated. I think I was in a state of shock.

"Exactly. He keeps hinting around at something much worse than stealing, doing that chopping again, smearing catsup around. No words needed to tell us something pretty grim. All right?"

"All right," I said.

"And if you can't raise anyone by signaling tomorrow morning, I want you to get on those seats and get out of here on the afternoon tide just as soon as it changes toward north. Take that lantern with you. It's watertight even if it is splashed. I put new batteries in it. If you drift west, you've got a good chance of bumping into a boat before dark. Then come back and get me. I'll be right here under this overhang."

I didn't answer him, thinking that I should tell him to wash his face. He'd feel better. I went on listening to him while heating our dinner, the beef stroganoff, but decided not to argue with him. There wasn't any use. Yet I had no intention of leaving Isla Dulce that way, without him, and every intention of trying to get his insulin back. Somehow. He wasn't capable of doing it himself.

"Thank God he didn't cut them up today," he went on.

"Cut what up?"

"The seats. Before you go to bed tonight be sure and let the air out of them. Then you can pump them up again tomorrow, and I'll strap them together, as I told you. We've got plenty of line."

"Okay," I said, playing along.

He was still nursing his ankle with the ice pack, talking calmly, if not wisely. "You'll be okay out there, Peg, I promise." But I think he was trying to convince himself, not me, that I'd make it.

"What about stripping all the boards off his

hut and making a raft big enough for both of us?"
I suggested.

"What does he do while we're tearing his
place down?"

"What can he do?"

"Swing that ax, that's what he can do. And
I can't run from him now. But you're right, we
could try and make a raft out of those boards—"
He stopped. "No. The key to this whole thing is
finding him and putting him out of business. I
knew that yesterday and I know it tonight."

"Do you mean to fight him?"

My father was slow in answering. "Put him
out of business some way . . ."

Kneeling by the fire, stirring the pot, pushing
back at the darkness of that thought, I said, "I
can't figure out how he knew we'd left here
today."

"He saw us from the ridgeline."

"But we looked up there."

"Not at the right place, that's obvious."

While I was making rice, I was thinking about
tomorrow. "Is the usual stuff in your kit?" He
knew what I meant—the insulin and syringes.

"Yes. But, hey, don't get any ideas."

"I was just thinking that if your ankle is better
in the morning, we might try to find those caves
and flush him out."

He looked over at me. "Peg, I've already thought about that, and if I can stand and walk, even halfway walk, well, that's exactly what I'll do. Flush him out."

But if you can't walk, what then, Daddy? I thought.

Twilight had come and gone, and we soon ate. We were ferociously hungry.

Then after I'd washed the dinner pans, he asked me to bring him two glass jars. The only ones we had held salad dressing and pickles.

"Empty them," he said.

Then he asked if I knew how to braid cloth. Of course I did. He'd seen my hair in braids now and then. "Okay, take that shirt he clobbered yesterday, cut some strips from it, and make me two thin braids about twelve inches long."

"What for?"

"I'll show you."

I went down to the tideline, dumped the stuff, and brought the empty jars back to him. "Wipe 'em dry with a paper towel," he instructed.

"What are you going to do?"

"I said I'd show you."

With that, he switched on the lantern, lighting up the overhang, making the stone walls friendly again. Crawling over to the spare gas can, he filled the two jars about three-quarters to the top, then extinguished the light, plunging us back into darkness.

"Last night while I was sitting here carving away, I tried to think of anything else we might have around to defend us in case he came down. I just can't see myself battling him with a butcher knife. I'm not made that way. In fact, it's a wonder I didn't stab myself in the gut when I fell today."

I sat there plaiting the strips of shirt, listening, thinking that he had finally decided to stop playing hide-and-seek games on Isla Dulce. I knew that whatever he was doing, those gasoline jars could kill.

He said, calmly, "So I've come up with something we can manufacture right here, just with what we've got; something I can throw at him from eight or ten feet. They're called Molotov cocktails, named after the Russian foreign minister during World War II. Russian soldiers tossed them at German tanks. They're quite easy to make."

After the flare of bright light, I couldn't see his face in the shadows, but there was satisfaction in his voice. He was pleased with himself, I could tell.

"They're simple enough, Peg. You just need some cloth or string for a fuse, and a bottle with thin glass; make sure you don't fill the gas all the way to the top, then light the thing and throw it. Fast! Get rid of it and duck. It makes a big bang."

I said, "Set him on fire?" *Burn him up?*

"That's right." His tone was matter-of-fact.

"We'll both carry matches. But I have to warn you that the little bombs are very dangerous. Sometimes Russian soldiers set themselves on fire by not getting rid of them in time. Just in case you have to do it, light and throw instantly. Remember that: light and throw. And if we're lucky, he'll be standing on rock, or near a boulder, so the 'cocktail' will shatter. Otherwise, we throw at his feet. . . ."

We were joining the psycho in insanity. We were going beyond talk and into action. We were planning to kill him if he attacked us.

I soon handed my father the two fuses, each about twelve inches long.

The lantern was switched on briefly once again as he opened the lids, tucked the cloth strips inside, and then tightly closed them, leaving about eight inches of cloth dangling. After he dipped the ends in motor oil, he crawled over to his sleeping bag to set them upright against the back wall, within arm's reach.

I could imagine what might happen if they had to be thrown—a man dancing around on fire. Burning alive as we watched.

The jars glistened in the yellow glow. I shuddered. Yes, we'd gone beyond talk.

The total blackness of early night had lifted a little, and the feast of stars visited us again, to turn the cove velvet gray. The cooking coals in the fire pit were still red. Sprawled out on his sleeping bag, ice pack again on his ankle, my father lit up an after-dinner pipe. Apple-scented tobacco smoke soon floated near the ceiling of the overhang. It should have been a serene time, a time to enjoy where we were. I tried to think of home and safety. I didn't want him to talk; I wanted to put all of what had happened out of my mind. But he talked anyway.

"Peg, it's just this, if it comes down to . . . If it's between you and that man, whoever he is, don't hesitate to use these jars. If I'm out of it, for any reason, save yourself. Don't be concerned about his life; think about yours."

I stayed silent.

He waited and then said, "Okay, I know what you're thinking and I'll put it flat out: the way he's acting, he's capable of rape, murder, torture, anything. So, if for any reason I'm not able to help you, don't let him get near you. Use them. Just make certain they break."

Finally I said, "I will," not knowing if I could.

After another long silence and a labored sigh, he said, "Now, the thing to do is have a little luck tonight and get some sleep. We'll see what's what in the morning. Hope this ankle's better."

I hoped so, too.

This time I was the one who walked out on the beach and shone the lantern beam all along the cliff brink, for what good it did. Isla Dulce seemed peaceful enough now. Maybe Señor Psycho had bedded down for the night.

Back under the overhang, I tucked into the sleeping bag, repeating the "Now I lay me down" prayer, feeling like a small child again, wanting to spiral off into sleep but afraid to. I was waiting for something to happen.

My father had drawn a blanket around his shoulders, over that ancient navy jacket, to combat the chill, determined to stay awake as long as possible; waiting, too, for the maniac to make himself known. Would he howl this night, throw something down?

After ten or fifteen minutes, I was still awake and turned my head as Father lit up again. The match flare and tobacco glow illuminated his face for a few seconds. I could see that it was tense and drawn, on edge, though the tone of his voice had been calm and collected. So he was as nervous as I was in that cove darkness.

"I've been thinking about some things," I said.

"What's the one right now?"

"About that time when I was in camp up near Big Bear, and we were outside at night. I was ten. Remember I went that year? Campfire Girls?"

"Um-huh."

"A counselor was telling us a ghost story, and she had another counselor run right by us, screaming her head off, wearing a white sheet. I told you about it when I came home. None of us slept that night. Not a wink."

"You did tell me."

Suddenly I began trembling uncontrollably, yet I wasn't cold. "I was terrified that night, Daddy. That's the way I feel right now, terrified. I go from being brave to being just terrified."

He reached over for my hand and held it.

Tears came quickly, and I babbled on that I was so afraid, that I didn't want to go out on those seats tomorrow, that I wanted to be home in bed. And why did he even come to this terrible island? Why did he bring me? My mother had been right. All of it came gushing out, everything I'd held in for two days. And underneath all that, I was really wanting him to be Sam Toland, the invincible—my hero—again. I wanted him to take my hand in the thunderstorm, ride the white horse, and slay the dragon. Kill the wacko himself, not leave the job to me.

After I'd quieted down, he said, "If it makes you feel any better, this is the worst thing that's ever happened to me, too. Worse than the war, worse than anything else. And I wish I was home in my bed, too. When that navy doctor told me I had diabetes, I thought my life was destroyed. Then when your mother divorced me, I felt discarded and unworthy, second-worst thing that ever happened to me. But this is a different kind of worst, and I'm ready to trade my life just to get you off here safely."

"I'm sorry I said all those things." I *was*, truly sorry. His life was in as much danger as mine, maybe more. I didn't have diabetes.

He sighed deeply. "I've been a fool all along, risking you out here, risking you in those other places. Your mother was right."

"No, she wasn't," I said. "I wanted to come here—always wanted to go with you. And if you think it's our best chance, I'll go out on those seats tomorrow."

He shook his head. "I won't let you. That's dumb desperation talk, I realize. I'm going up after him tomorrow and I'm going to try to kill him, even if I have to do it on a crutch."

I didn't answer. Exhausted from words and fear, I fell asleep.

A little later, I awakened both of us with a scream. It was the first of many nightmares. Big hands were reaching for me under the overhang. I could smell his sour breath.

CHAPTER FOURTEEN

Tuesday Morning

FEELING STIFF AND GROGGY, a gritty mess, my hair tangled, I awakened not long before sunup and leaned over toward my father, glad to see that he was still asleep. On top of his bag, not in it. He'd crawled over to the tent during the night for another blanket. He was all bunched up in two of them and had probably stayed awake for hours.

Best of all, nothing had happened to us during the night. Nothing had been thrown down on us. No howls. No games. No terror. No harassing of any kind.

I stayed in the bag a while longer, looking at the figure in the bunched blankets, knowing that he was supposed to have an insulin shot very soon; knowing also that he wouldn't have one at all. I was worried about that.

Finally I got up to face the day, whatever it

might bring, and went to the bathroom on the far side of the cove, then came back to start the fire and boil water for coffee. Light grew slowly, dapple gray on the edges, though it looked as if there would soon be another pretty cobalt sky above.

All the while, I was trying to think of what he'd told me long ago about diabetic coma: Likely, he'd be irritable before it happened; his speech might become slurred, his skin dry. There'd be weakness and maybe vomiting. A lot of thirst. Deep and rapid breathing. When the coma stage came, it might seem like a light sleep. After a while, the coma might become deep. More or less, he'd repeated all the symptoms to me several times over the years.

"Never, never try to pour liquids down a diabetic's throat. You can end up suffocating him." I well remembered the warning about that.

I also remembered that on these trips he always took along something in the big shaving kit called glucagon. If he went into insulin shock, from too much insulin, that solution could be used to bring him out. The mixture was to be injected by needle and syringe. I'd never given him a shot; I'd never even seen him take a shot, and I'd had no desire to do so. Yet it was a never-ending part of his life.

What he faced now was something called hyperglycemia, too little insulin, always worse than shock.

"You usually come out of shock in a matter of hours, anyway. Nature does it. The real danger is if you have heart trouble or some other complication."

So far as I knew, my father had a sound heart, the heart of a strong horse.

Getting the insulin back from the crazy man was the problem; finding the kit somewhere up on the island top was the problem; finding *him* was the problem.

By sunup, I had the water boiling and was sipping coffee when my father slowly, fitfully awakened. He sat up. His eyes were bloodshot and puffy, white gunk in the corners. He now had a four-day growth of beard and looked as if he should be in a hospital, not stranded on a forgotten island.

"How do you feel?"

"I don't know yet," he answered, staring bleakly at me.

"How's the ankle?"

"It hurts like hell, Peg. Get me the shovel, will you?"

I got it for him. He crawled out and rose unsteadily, putting all his weight on his right foot.

"Do you need help?"

"No." He hobbled off pitifully to go to the bathroom, using the shovel as a makeshift crutch.

Watching Sam Toland, always the proud man, move slowly and painfully across the sand, head bent, all fight out of him, was crushing. He'd been beaten down by someone he hadn't even seen. I realized how remarkable that was: This man had terrorized us and beaten us down without ever touching us, without ever saying a word to us, without our knowing why any of it had happened. Sam Toland could now die on Isla Viernes Dulce and not know why. I could die that way, too.

Returning to the overhang, he slipped under and lowered himself to his bag again, gritting his teeth. I then saw his foot for the first time since the previous evening. Blue-black around the knob of the anklebone, it was badly swollen. The ice pack hadn't helped very much. The diabetic's fear of foot injury had come true.

For sure, there'd be no walking around on top for him today. The maniac wouldn't be "put out of business" by Sam Toland today. It was S. J. Toland who was out of business.

I think he knew it. He looked weak and sullen, angry at the whole world, like a sick, cornered lion.

"I'm getting breakfast for you," I said, wanting to strike a positive note.

"No breakfast. I'm not hungry!" He was staring at me. "I need some water. Hurry."

I nodded. Hurrying was exactly what I was doing. I wanted to get up on that top and begin sending an SOS. But I was also wondering how long it would take for his system to react to the lack of both the evening and morning shots. At the same time, I was afraid to ask; I really didn't want to know.

"Can't I make you some coffee?"

"Yes," he barked.

"Do I put sugar in?"

"No."

He was already sweating, I saw, even though the morning was still chilly. I was guessing that all the stress, plus the ankle, was compounding the lack of insulin.

I ate breakfast about ten minutes later, just juice and toast, watching him constantly. He seemed to be dozing, but his breathing was shallow and rapid.

I finished, and after walking down to the tideline to scan the cliff, I said, "I'll clean up when I get back," and lifted the butcher knife from beside his bag.

He eyed me dully. "Where are you going with that?"

"Up on top. To signal."

"Listen to me. Don't ever put your back to him. Stand sideways up there so the rotten SOB can't sneak up on you and push you over. Watch out for him."

I bent down and kissed his hot, moist forehead; then I picked up the "signaling pan" and went topside up the crawlway, pan hanging from my belt, knife in my right hand. It is surprising, but not recommended, how you can use parts of your hands, your knuckles, and your wrists to gain traction on loose dirt.

Reaching the top, I looked around very carefully, edging higher to look up-island. I couldn't see *him* anywhere, and I settled down to the right of the crawlway, sitting on the dirt sideways, staying near the edge so that I could take a couple of side rolls and go down, if need be.

I wiped the bottom of the pan clean and began flashing it seaward and eastward. The morning, once again, was lovely—intense blue sky, rising warm sun, whisper of breeze.

Not long afterward, I heard the maddening buzz of those same outboard motors from over toward Boca. They were probably still fifteen miles away, but the sound carried clearly, as it had done yesterday. Using my wrist to turn the pan, as my father had done, I made the SOS again and again in the direction of the sound.

Eventually the buzz died away, and I turned the pan more north to keep blinking it toward the cantina. I wondered whether or not a sun blink could be seen thirty miles away. But it was worth the try—anything was.

About nine o'clock I went back down the crawlway and saw that my father was asleep again on top of his bag. On his side, mouth partially open. I noticed that his hands were trembling slightly as he breathed in and out.

There was no need to awaken him as I went about cleaning up the breakfast mess, straightening up the camp in general. I also needed to do some personal things for myself, just repair work; as much as I could do without the makeup kit. Little things were getting to me. No toothbrush or toothpaste. No face soap. Combing my hair with my fingers, for instance, hating *him* with every stroke.

I washed my face again with a palmful of fresh water, then rubbed some olive oil into my cheeks and across my forehead. My skin was beginning to crocodile in the sun and breeze. I knew I looked awful. After taking care of myself, I felt better.

About an hour later I decided to awaken my father and talk about what we might do for the rest of the day, aside from signaling. I'd thought about staying up there all afternoon, waiting for any boat that might pull close enough to spot the flashes. I thought he might have some other ideas. Physically, he was of no help now, but his mind was still good. He knew a lot of things about surviving.

I touched his shoulder and shook it gently. He made no sound. "Daddy," I said several times. I shook him harder, yelling for him to wake up, demanding it. Finally his eyes opened and he said, blinking up at me, "Thass a twenny-ton load. . . ." Or that's what I thought he said. He was confused, delirious, useless. He was out of it, and slipping toward diabetic coma. Perhaps death. His eyes closed again.

For a while I just sat there in the cove looking at him, losing hope, wondering if what he'd said was really true—that he'd eventually wake up without medical help. Or would he just sleep on into death? I couldn't let that happen so easily, I thought. I touched his forehead. It was as dry as desert sand.

Then I thought about pumping up those two seats, strapping them together as he'd planned to do, tying him on them so he'd drift with the current, as he'd suggested I do myself. Then all sorts of negatives rose in my mind—his slipping off the seats, unconcious; the patches coming loose in the waves; the seats separating. Yes, the sharks. There was too much risk that way. It was truly "dumb desperation."

I sat there past noon looking at him, unable to avoid seeing the terrible fused jars of gasoline, which were only a few inches from his head. They appeared so innocent resting against the wall with their clear liquid, but I knew, or thought I knew, what they could do.

By that time I think I also knew what had to be done to that man who lived somewhere north of the cove. There was no other way.

Finally I asked myself if I could kill another human. Though I'd thought about it, turned it over in my mind, I don't think I'd seriously considered it until this awful moment. Could I kill in defense of someone I dearly loved and then live with that murder? At the last moment, the last second, would I say "I can't do it"?

I took another look at my father and stood.

CHAPTER FIFTEEN

Tuesday Afternoon

WITH THE MATCHES tucked into my shirt pocket, I wrapped the shining jars, with their limp fuses, in two pieces of torn toweling and placed them in my miniknapsack. If I happened to fall, it would probably be forward, not backward.

Then I checked my father again. The trembling in his hands had ceased; he was now deathly still, though his breathing was the same. I put my face down to his nose and also felt his chest going up and down. His breath was sickly sweet. Never having been around anyone unconscious from this sort of thing, I didn't know what to expect.

Along with the phony gun, I decided to carry the knife but not to use the sheath that was still on my father's belt. It was a miracle that he hadn't cut himself with the long, naked blade when he tumbled down. The only good thing about that long, shining blade was that it looked very mean and dangerous. Even held in *my* hands, it looked mean and dangerous.

I believe it was about one o'clock when I went up the crawlway; the sun was just past overhead, still drilling the top of the island. It was a cloudless noon hour, a noon hour when the sea was flat and oily. A beautiful midday. The morning's whisper of warm breeze was still passing across from the mainland.

Oddly enough, I was not overly afraid at this particular point. I guess the two days of harassment had drained me of most feeling. Thankfully, I'd reached a mental tiredness that was good for me, like a runner reaching the state where mind separates from body and movement is automatic.

Him?

I still thought of him as big, with dark, cold eyes. That hadn't changed. But I dwelt more on his hands now. I had no idea what his face would be like, but I had a clear picture of reaching hands. I didn't want him to touch my body. At the same time, I was trying to think of him as completely crazed, subhuman, so that whether he lived or died would not make a great difference to me.

I could imagine what I looked like up on the island top—jeans and shirt dirty, hair a mess, face smudged with dust from climbing the crawlway,

138

a weird-looking teenager holding a long knife and a rifle that looked real. Had I encountered that wild-looking girl, I'd have run the other way. *Fast*.

I looked around up on the brink for a moment or two, did not see him, and hurried north along the dirt, but not for long. We'd come this same path the day before; and from somewhere, he'd watched us, had known exactly when to visit the cove and do his damage. I reasoned that he might be watching me from up on the ridge right now.

So, about a quarter mile up-island, with the birds flying off, cackling and cawing, dropping dung up ahead of me, I found an alley down to the sea shelf, a spillway worn smooth by years of winter rains. I went down with my front to it, on my hands and knees, rubber soles braking me easily. Aside from a few places up ahead where the pieces of slab wall had fallen away to rest on the shelf, it looked passable all the way. The going would be slippery, though.

There were dozens of sea lions sunning up ahead, and the trumpeting began in earnest as they spotted me. They dove into the sea, about a foot down, as I approached. The huge bewhiskered bulls, roaring in foghorn voices, stared at me defiantly. Then they also flopped over into the water, following the females and younger males.

My father would have loved all this, I thought. He hadn't had the chance to walk it because of Señor Psycho.

Just the shelf alone he would have loved. Ten to twenty or thirty feet wide, it was home to hundreds of small tide pools. The whole thing was alive and quivering. Eelgrass wavered and danced; tiny sponges pulsated. Eel-like blennies and worms and crabs and starfish were in the pools, along with tiny, darting, rainbow-colored fish. Sea anemones waited patiently for their meals. Father had taught me to identify most of the reef creatures, but I had no time for them this day.

As I picked my way along the barnacle-crusted or algae-covered black rocks, I could see occasional tide caves, flooded at high water for certain, but happy homes to sea lion harems at low tide. This was all what my father had hoped to explore— the grottos especially.

My hatred for Psycho and what he'd done to us grew with each step forward.

Once, I stopped to look back. The sea lions were already crawling out of the water, recapturing their homes, bulls bleating to females to return immediately to the harems.

The broad shelf soon ended. I looked around for a way to climb back to the top, then go up on the ridge, thinking I was about level with where his camp would be located across the island. Then I noticed a narrower, higher ledge that seemed to go around the end of Sweet Friday. It appeared that some of the facing had fallen off into the sea, leaving a ledge two or three feet wide.

Going slowly, I inched out on it, worried about falling off. Water was lapping about ten feet below, and I crabbed sideways, holding the wooden gun in my right hand, the knife in my left. I'd gone about ten or fifteen yards when suddenly rock and dirt cascaded down from above, hitting my head and shoulders. There was a few seconds' warning, and I managed to duck most of it, putting my cheek to the cliff wall; but the knife slipped out of my hand and plunged into the sea.

Gripping the rifle tighter, I didn't attempt to move for several seconds, and then I looked up but could see nothing. The tumbling dirt could have been a coincidence. Rock and dirt slides do occur without people starting them. *Yet . . .*

I'd lost the knife but really didn't want it anyway. If my father thought he'd be no match in using it on that man, I'd be much less a knife fighter. I still had the two jars of gasoline, and I decided to go on.

Two or three minutes later the ledge ended abruptly, but there was an easy crawlway from it to the cliff top at that end. There were hand- and footprints all over it, so he'd been using it as well. I stared at his handprint. It wasn't as large as a catcher's mitt, the way I'd thought it would be. But it was large enough. I went on up.

In a few seconds I found myself looking down on his camp. Repeat of yesterday—no sign of him!

Yard by yard I looked over that rectangle to see if anything had changed. The only thing that seemed to be missing was the shirt on the line. He'd recaptured that belonging. The place was kind of eerie—no movement at all. It was as if I were looking at a still picture.

Though I could faintly hear the trumpeting and roaring of the sea lions, and the distant squawk and caw of birds, the heavy quiet of the little plateau sent the day's first real tremor of fear up from my stomach.

I studied the hut for a long time and decided he wasn't inside. *I hoped he wasn't inside.* I also thought that the only chance I might have with him would be to make him come to me, make him chase me up the ridge; and when he was close enough, and climbing, to throw the gas bombs down on him like firecrackers. I believed I could scramble up on the other side of the spring, where we'd come down yesterday, and keep ahead of him fifty or sixty feet, then slow down, turn around, and do it.

Do it! I hoped I'd have the courage to *do it*.

But to make him chase me, I knew I had to do something to him, make him angry. I finally decided to set his hut on fire. That canvas flap would likely burn after some gas was poured on it. I couldn't think of anything else to do.

I took my time thinking about it, almost seeing it happen: *Go down, light the fire, move away from the hut toward the spring, and wait for him to run at me. Then go up the slope, turn around and wait. Light one jar and throw it; hold the other one and throw it only if I had to.*

All of it depended on whether or not he'd chase me.

A few minutes later, holding the rifle out in front of me, I went down the steep bank on my rear end. Once down, I walked slowly up to the hut, scarcely taking a breath, just holding everything inside me. I finally used the barrel of the wooden gun to push aside the flap. Nothing was in the hut. No shaving kit. None of our belongings.

He was nowhere to be seen. I moved back and looked around again, sensing now that his eyes were on me. It was the exact same feeling that I'd had in the cove Sunday morning, when my father claimed it was all a false alarm. Eyes, very angry eyes, were on me now, I was certain. From where, I didn't know.

I thought, *Okay, come on. Do it. Right now or never. No more games.*

I poured some gasoline—just enough to wet it—on the canvas flap, secured the bottle and fuse in my knapsack, then carefully lit the flap and went quickly over to the spring area to wait for him. Flames began to travel upward, burning brightly but with little smoke.

For the next two or three minutes, I was wishing I had ten sets of eyes to cover every inch of that little mesa, to spot him the moment he moved.

By now burning pieces of the flap had begun to fall to earth and the wooden frame had caught fire. More smoke was rising over Sweet Friday.

What happened next was movement on the other side of the ravine, down at the bottom of the rectangle where my father had stopped yesterday and refused to go on. I caught it in the corner of my eye and went out beyond the hut just in time to see a man's back and a straw hat. He was wearing a blue shirt and he bobbed *away* from me, not toward me, running jerkily, awkwardly.

It took a moment for me to realize that he wasn't going to chase me. I couldn't understand that, since it upset everything I'd planned to do.

Why isn't he chasing me? He could see I was alone near his burning hut.

Not sure of what to do now, I ran toward the ravine, following him, hoping to get a better look at him, but he'd already disappeared down-island, through the brush, which was heavier on this west side. I knew, from yesterday, that the only quick way to cross the deep crevice was to get a running start and jump the six or eight feet. My father was right, he couldn't have made it.

I backed up, took a good grip on the rifle, and sailed over the ravine easily, landing on my feet, hoping that he was still moving south—not hiding, ready to jump me. But there weren't many places to hide up there in that knee-high brush.

Hesitating a moment on the lip of the ravine, I spotted a path on which he'd probably moved, and then I began to go along it at a slow, slow walk—heart slamming, each breath hurting with fear now that I'd actually seen him. Whatever small bravery I'd had near his camp was quickly leaving me, slipping away with each step.

He'd used the path a lot. Brush was ground down and pushed along the narrow trail. The dirt in it was well trampled. His boot heels had been all over it. Finally the trail veered off sharply toward the ridgeline, then went over a small hillock. In a moment I was stopped dead in my tracks, fighting pure panic.

Ahead was the unmistakable dark hole of a cave mouth, one of those described in the Hydrographic Office publication. Set in gray rock, with brush around it, the entrance was about a yard in diameter, hands-and-knees entry only.

I stood about fifty feet away, not knowing what to do now. Nothing was going as I'd planned. I believed he was inside that hole, yet I couldn't understand why he'd ducked in there, why he'd run from me. Just plain, ordinary common sense would tell him not to get trapped in a cave.

Yet he'd seen the rifle and could be thinking it was real—that I'd shoot him if I could get a bead on him. So that was why he was hiding!

Of course, there was also the good possibility that he wasn't in there at all, that he'd gone on to the cove and had found my father unconscious. Had used the ax on him.

Just as bad, he'd circled around behind me!

I didn't make a move for several minutes. Would my father, at this point, call out and try to talk to him? In my shoes, would he do that? The answer was no.

I thought about using one of the jars—lighting it, throwing it inside. *Boom!* If he was in there, great. If he wasn't, I'd still have a jar left.

What kept picking at me all this time was the danger of getting caught from behind some way, having him sneak up and grab me with those hands that I'd built into great clutching claws.

I stood a moment longer, finally realizing that my legs and hands were quivering, knowing that I had to do something or run back to the cove. I'd never have the courage again to come up here.

What would Sam Toland, my hero, have done right now? I had to think that he wouldn't take any more chances with this silent, unseen wacko. He'd said that, several times.

I went forward about another twenty feet and eased the gas jars out of the knapsack. I tightened the lids on both, put one on the ground for spare, and walked up another five feet.

"Do it now," I said to myself. "Now!" Kill him and find the insulin kit.

Crossing my fingers mentally, holding my breath, I lit the oil-soaked fuse and lobbed the jar into the entrance of the cave.

Next thing I knew I was on the ground, spun around and knocked down by the thundering blue-red blast. I'd had no idea it would be that powerful. I was on my hands and knees, and my ears were ringing. My face felt singed.

The brush around the cave entrance was burning, and the smoke, oddly enough, was being sucked inside——but no big, black-bearded, cold-eyed maniac came staggering out, coughing and half-blinded. The only sound was the sharp crackling of the creosote bushes.

Staying on my hands and knees, I went back to the other bottle, matches ready in case he did come crawling out. I stayed on my knees a long time, watching the round dark hole, looking at the whitish gray smoke twisting up into the Cortez sky, suddenly thinking that was what we should have done on Sunday——set that useless two-thousand-dollar Redshank on fire. Even jet aircraft would have seen that black smoke.

According to my watch, almost a half hour had passed. The brush had burned out, and smoke was no longer being sucked into the cave. *Finally*, I thought. *You must do it. You must go in there and look for that shaving kit.*

Now wishing I hadn't dropped the knife, I went up slowly and carefully, staying to one side in case he rushed out. Nearing the cave, I saw my cologne bottle, now empty. Near it was an after-shave bottle, also empty. It was the same brand my father used.

At the entrance I delayed at least five minutes before sticking just the top of my head and eyes down to look in——not much of a target for him. The smell of burned brush and gasoline was thick around the torched entrance. The dark of the cave was broken by what seemed to be a small oblong of light deep inside.

It took several minutes more to work up the courage to enter the space. I left the big-banging little gas bomb just outside, hidden beyond the oval entrance, but took the matches. Again barely breathing, I crawled in.

A few feet inside I struck a match and in the flare saw a body stretched out at the far end of the cave, near that oblong of light—an air hole. That's why the smoke had been sucked in. A straw hat was where the man's head should be. I breathed relief. At least I knew where he was. The match went out.

I lit another and looked around. I saw the red-handled ax, the gaff, my open makeup bag, our fishing rods, and finally my father's shaving kit. I also became aware of a sweetish smell in there.

A third match revealed that crowded into the dark hole were pots and pans, food, clothing, a mattress, and a blanket. Whoever this beach bum or sea gypsy was, this was where he'd been living temporarily.

Then I realized what that other smell was, beside the strong odor of burned gas and smoke. My own cologne was heavy in that cave; perhaps the shaving lotion, too. He must have tried to deodorize his hole in the ground. He qualified for "Psycho," all right.

I lit a fourth match and held it in the direction of the body. It was too shadowy to make out anything about him except his shirt, pants, straw hat, and cowboy boots. He wasn't tall enough to be Raul Clemente. I thought he was dead and decided to go no closer.

A final match was just enough to allow me time to retrieve the red-handled ax and check the shaving kit for the syringes and insulin solutions.

Ax and kit in hand, I backed out, picked up the gas jar, and began to run toward the cove along the west side of Sweet Friday Island. I didn't want to think about what I'd done. Not now, at least. My father needed medicine.

As I ran I was aware of only two things: great thirst and lack of wind. I was totally parched and couldn't suck enough air down into my lungs. I realize now all this was caused by coming down from a mountain of sustained fear.

CHAPTER SIXTEEN
The Insulin Shot

WRAPPED AROUND THE two small glucagon bottles in my father's kit were the typed instructions on how to use them; but glucagon didn't apply here, and he had not written down anything about the dosage of insulin. I tried to remember what he took each morning. I knew it was measured in units. Twenty? Thirty? Forty?

I didn't see much change in him over the past two hours. He was asleep, and even looked as if he might be enjoying it. His face was red, but the tension and tiredness seemed to have gone. I thought he was dying.

Of all the people I knew anywhere, I certainly wasn't the one to do this job. I always felt queasy just seeing syringes. It was the idea of it, inserting the needle into the skin, more than the pain of it.

He partially awakened, mumbled something

unintelligible, then closed his eyes again. His lips moved, but nothing came out.

It took a minute to tug the navy jacket off and roll up my father's sleeve so that I could reach the fatty part under his right arm, an area recommended by the glucagon instructions. I could also inject his stomach, the way he did. The latter was best, the instructions said. Not for me!

I sat for a little while, wondering what would happen if I gave him the wrong dosage. Too much? Too little?

Not knowing what a unit of insulin was or how to measure it, I finally decided to fill the syringe three-quarters full and gamble that that would be enough.

Remembering what happened to me when I took shots, I wiped the area under his arm with alcohol-dipped cotton, pinched up the skin, and then, forcing myself to keep my eyes wide open, pushed the needle into his arm and drained the entire syringe. I wiped the tiny blood-dotted hole with the cotton and rolled his sleeve back down. He made no sound or movement throughout the whole thing.

I rose, walked a few feet, and fainted dead away.

CHAPTER SEVENTEEN

An Ermitaño

WHILE WAITING FOR my father to recover, I set fire to the Redshank by pouring gasoline over it. Soon gray-black smoke was coiling up out of Isla Viernes Dulce Cove, high into the feathery blue sky. If only we'd done that two days before. The coil stood out like a great black snake against the blueness.

Next I ate. I was starved, and I gulped food down but threw it up in a few minutes. What I had done in the cave was just sinking in, and I felt nauseous and had trouble breathing. I kept seeing that body in the shadows by the air hole.

About an hour later I heard a murmur from my father and went over to him. He was licking his lips, pursing them, running his tongue over them. Eyes opened, closed; opened, closed. He didn't know where he was, blinking and trying to focus.

I said, "Daddy, you'll be okay," watching him closely.

He nodded and looked around, finally realizing he was still under the overhang on Sweet Friday.

"I have the insulin. I got it back."

He was still groggy and didn't really understand.

I sat beside him and held his hand for a while. Eventually he opened his eyes again and looked over, saying, "Helluva thing I did to you, conking out that way."

"You didn't mean to."

He nodded agreement. "No, I didn't." He seemed to be very weak; each movement was difficult.

I asked, "Can you swallow okay?"

"I think so." He closed his eyes and swallowed.

"Are you thirsty?"

He nodded.

I gave him some water and said, "I hope I did the right thing. I filled the syringe three-quarters with insulin."

He frowned. "You gave me a shot? Where did you get it?" His speech was slurred.

"From *him*."

He frowned and blinked, eyes following the

black rope of smoke into the sky. He was dazed. "How?" he asked. "He had the kit."

"I found it in a cave. He was living there, I think."

"How did you get it back? Talk him out of it?"

"No, not that way."

Then I told him everything, even saying that I'd killed the man.

He reached for my hand, shaking his head, saying, "No, no, no. Why you? Why didn't I do it the other day? Oh, Peg, I'm so sorry."

Still holding my hand, he closed his eyes, and tears trickled down from them. Then he swallowed and took hold of himself, saying, "Give me a while to get some of my strength back, and I'll go on up there. I want to see him."

I didn't want him to do that, even if he was capable of it. All I wanted to do was leave the island. Leave everything and go. Leave *him* like he was. Maybe no one would ever know, or care, except us.

I had thought about the Mexican police while my father was waking up, and now I asked, "Will we have to tell the police?"

"Of course we will. *I will*. Not you."

"But I did it."

He turned his head toward me. "You listen. You're going to do exactly what I say. I'm responsible for him, not you. No matter what, he's my responsibility. I made the Molotov cocktails; you didn't. I used them on him; you didn't. I'll tell them I went up there and killed him because he threatened our lives again and again. It was him or us, and they'll understand that once they see the rocks and the pictures of what he did to the Redshank—"

I said, "Daddy—"

Alarm in his bloodshot eyes, he said, "Listen to me, Peg, dammit, listen. We're in a foreign country. Just because we're next door to California doesn't mean anything. I just hope that man up there is American. I'll find out soon."

"What difference does it make?" I asked, a void where my stomach was. *I'd killed someone*, and that message kept repeating in the back of my head. I didn't think he was American, from the way he was dressed.

"In a Mexicali court, it may make a big difference, believe me."

"Don't go to the police," I pleaded.

"Peg, it'll be worse if we don't."

My head spun and spun. I just wanted to vanish.

He tightened his grip on my hand, saying,

"It'll work out okay for us, I promise. Let's think about feeding that fire." He was slowly beginning to recover.

The Redshank was now a pile of writhing, bubbling chemicals, blackened and shrinking. Soon it would be just a foul burned spot on the sand.

"Go up and throw down all the brush you can to keep it burning."

By this time the black smoke coil was at least a mile high, and almost any boat or aircraft in the upper Cortez could see it. Sooner or later someone who knew the island was uninhabited would investigate—maybe the police from San Felipe.

We didn't have to wait too long. At about four o'clock, when I was tossing down creosote brush, I heard the sharp banging of an outboard and looked south. A big fishing skiff was swinging out wide, avoiding the east string of rocks, setting a course to drive it into the cove. I scrambled down.

My father had heard the engine racket, too, and had the binoculars trained on the skiff. He said, "It's them."

"Who is them?"

He passed the glasses. Erect in the stern was Raul Clemente, and in front of him, a dark-bloused lump—unmistakably the old woman.

157

I returned the glasses, and my father took another look but made no comment.

I went down to the waterline as the banging of the engine grew louder and finally became deafening in the cove, volleying and rolling off the cliff face. I stood and waited for them, aware of anger not only in their outboard but in their faces.

Clemente cut the racketing outboard thirty feet away, and the heavy boat arrowed in, prow driving far up on the sand. Both Clemente and the old crone were staring at us. He yelled, "You two! I warned you not to come out here. You lied to me, you didn't go to Piño."

Weary, ill, face white with rage, lying on his back, my father was in no mood to take anything off Clemente. "Why didn't you tell us the truth? There's a madman out here."

Clemente looked over our heads, scanning the cliff top. Then his eyes dropped back to the beach and the boulders, still burning, smoking fire. Then he jumped out of the boat, throwing the anchor far up on the sand.

"Where is he?" Clemente asked, glaring at us.

"Up there in a cave," my father said. "I think he's dead. And if you want to know who killed him, Clemente—I did."

There was a sharp cry from the old woman, and they both ran for the crawlway. She went up as if she were a child, Clemente following on her heels. He only paused a moment to frown at the pit with the glass shards sticking up from it.

My father, shaking all over, shouted after them, "I hope he's dead. Do you hear that? I hope he's dead." Then, anger spent, he sighed deeply. "That's how I feel; I don't care about him."

"What do we do now?" I asked.

He looked up. "We wait for them, Margaret. That's what we do. We wait right here. If that guy up there is someone they know, so what? I don't care."

A moment later, he stared at Clemente's boat. "We should steal their damn boat and go."

That would have been just fine with me. I never wanted to see them again, nor any of Baja.

About ten minutes later we heard voices from above, speaking Spanish. We waited.

Finally they appeared on the cliff top near the crawlway—Clemente, the old woman, and someone else, *him*, Señor Psycho, in person. He was leaning on Clemente.

I couldn't believe it. *He was alive, alive.*

They were talking to him in Spanish, speaking softly.

My father said, "Oh, my God, Peg, he's old. Look how old he is."

For a few seconds, nothing registered with

me. *I haven't killed anybody,* was what I was thinking—was the only thing I was thinking. Then,
finally, I did see how very old he was. Maybe in
his seventies. His straw hat was cocked back, and
we could see milk-white silky hair and parchment
skin. His cheeks were sunken. I now realized why
the man I'd seen run away from the ravine moved
so jerkily, so awkwardly—it was an old man's
run.

Some things were falling into place. What he'd
done—stabbing the boat, the spiders, the boulders, stealing the kits—was the work of a bad
child or someone senile.

About that time the old man spotted my father
and began jabbering wildly in Spanish, pointing,
pulling back from the edge of the cliff, obviously
frightened by us. Clemente calmed him, and then
they began helping him down the crawlway.

I saw that the back of his shirt was scorched
and knew that the explosion had done that to
him. He could have been fried if he'd been near
the cave entrance.

I moved toward the crawlway to help them
but the old crone screamed at me, *"Cesar, cesar!"*
She was all hatred.

My father said, "She doesn't want your help."

That was evident. I shrugged and moved back.
They managed to move the old man by the

sand pit, skirting it, and then came past us, supporting him. Trembling all over, his eyes were wide, like those of a frightened doe. His toothless, quivering mouth was in an O. Straggly white whiskers were dotted over his sunken cheeks. I'd seen people like him in rest homes. I'll never forget how he looked as he went by us in shadowy Sweet Friday Cove.

They put him down in the front seat of the skiff, and the crone sat beside him, speaking to him, putting her arm around him, cooing to him, comforting him as if we were criminals.

Clemente walked over. "What were you doing out here? What's the pit for? I saw a wooden rifle up by the cave. Are you two crazy?"

My father, still sitting in the sand, looked up at him. "Yeah, we're crazy, Clemente."

Clemente went on angrily. "You almost killed him, a helpless old man. His shirt is all scorched. His back is burned. What did you do to him? You chased him into that cave? He was so frightened he couldn't move. He was paralyzed from fear. His face was in that air hole. I had to pull him away."

My father went on his own attack. "Yeah, we're crazy, Clemente. The first two hours we were here, that idiot slashed our boat and stole our ax; then he threw spiders on me. . . ."

161

"He was frightened of you, that's all," Clemente shouted back. "He's nothing but a helpless old *ermitano,* a hermit."

My father raged on, not really listening to Clemente. ". . . chopped up my daughter's clothes, destroyed our water jugs. That's what the pit was for—to keep a madman away from us."

"He was frightened of you," Clemente lashed back.

My father pointed to the smoldering boat remains. "Your dumb hermit did that."

They'd each spent their rage, it seemed; and in a moment, Clemente said quietly, "I told you not to come here."

My father quieted down, too. He sighed, "You didn't say why." He was totally exhausted.

Clemente didn't answer that but took a long, deep breath and looked all around the cove. "Whatever you want to take from here, put it in the boat."

He even helped me load the skiff, carrying the Mercury himself. My father couldn't help us.

Throughout all that I noticed that the old man's wide, doe eyes stayed on my father; and the old woman looked daggers at both of us. But she'd done that even before we came out to Sweet Friday. She just didn't like Americans, I thought.

Clemente said nothing the whole time we

were loading the boat. When we were finished, the camp struck and nothing left behind, I helped my father hobble over to sit down on the seat next to the stern. Clemente took his seat by the engine, and I jumped in last, after shoving the boat off.

Clemente backed down and then made a circle as we pounded out of the cove. I looked past him to the black spot on the beach where the Redshank had been cremated. I looked at the prehistoric boulders, like the ones cavemen used to stun dinosaurs. In the shadows I couldn't see the tin-can gondola warning line. Nor could I see the glass-shard jungle pit.

I turned to look forward and saw the bent, scorched back of the man that I thought I'd killed. Even his straw hat had been scorched by the blast.

The strange, silent human cargo in the skiff began to cross the Sea of Cortez toward Boca de Cangrejo. A mile or so off, I turned again to look at Isla Viernes Dulce. It sat awash in calm dignity, looking inviting, as most islands do at a distance. Sweet Friday hadn't really changed a pebble since Sunday, but we had changed. Part of us, a dark part, would always be there under the overhang, sitting in terror.

CHAPTER EIGHTEEN
Tuesday Night

NIGHT HAD SETTLED down over the Cortez, and the few lights of Boca were cutting it with orange glows when Clemente beached the skiff directly in front of the Toyota Land Cruiser. Never did any vehicle look so good as that one. Waiting patiently for us, intact, it looked strong enough to go to the moon.

No sooner had we set foot on land than Clemente said to my father, "Leave here as soon as you can." It was more advice than threat.

"Don't worry," my father answered, moving slowly toward the four-wheel drive, dragging his lame foot. He was very weak.

Clemente pulled the skiff out again and took his ancient passengers up in front of the cantina. I saw them disappear inside.

Clemente came back to hoist the Mercury on the Land Cruiser roof and tie it.

I quickly unloaded everything else out on the sand and began to load the Cruiser. My father took time to eat some bread and drink some orange juice, staring around vacantly. He needed to be in the hospital.

A few minutes later, just before I climbed into the Toyota, where my father was already waiting, motor running, lights on, Clemente trudged up out of the darkness.

My father asked, "Who was that old man? What's his story?"

Clemente answered, "I told you, a hermit. Now, please leave here and never come back."

My father laughed in a brittle way. "Who would ever want to come back here?"

And so we gladly left little, lost Boca, with its few people and flickering firelights, and started across the Gran Desierto in the blackest of the night, headed for Mexico 2 and the border.

Though I wasn't licensed yet, I'd driven stick shift but never one like the Toyota's. "Put it in second and keep it there," said S. J. Toland, and that's the way we went to El Centro.

We didn't talk very much, and the headlights picked up nothing but the silent, eerie desert. But both of us were thinking a lot about an old man whom I'd almost killed.

At the emergency room of the hospital in El Centro, the young doctor on duty asked, "Whatever happened to you two?"

"We went camping," said my father, as they wheeled him to X-ray to check the ankle.

CHAPTER NINETEEN
A Long Time Later

NO ONE THINKS of anything constantly, but the old man whose toothless mouth made an O, whose eyes grew large and full of dread at the sight of my father, kept coming back at me at odd times over the years. I thought, off and on, about Sweet Friday Island and Easter week and the trembling old man, in my waking hours and in violent nightmares.

Sometimes I was trapped under the overhang, and he'd come in howling and swinging the red-handled ax; other times he was in the cave and always dead when I'd roll him over, the mouth wide open and locked in that O. Sometimes I awakened myself with screams. Sometimes I awakened others. That noise is not appreciated at 2:00 A.M.

I tried to talk to my father now and then about the old man from Boca de Cangrejo, especially after I'd had a nightmare. But he always avoided more than a few words, always changed the subject. I believe he wanted to bury, forever, the memory of those four shattering days and nights on Sweet Friday Island. I believe he thought he'd failed me.

The last time I tried, I said, "Why won't you talk about it?"

He replied, almost angrily, "Because I don't want to, Peg." Then silence fell in that apartment, and I never mentioned the island again.

I was always certain that there was a connection between Raul Clemente, the old man, and the woman in black; that there had to be an explanation for what had happened on Sweet Friday Island. Helpless, harmless old "hermit" I did not buy.

The nightmares continued through high school and into college. They'd go away for months, then suddenly come back; hide in some deep recess of my brain, then slip out to explode in a repeat of Cortez terror.

Finally, in my senior year of college, I went to a psychiatrist. We talked about it over several sessions. I told her that in many dreams I'd actually killed the old man, saw him burning head to foot.

"But you were trying to protect your father—keep him *alive*—that's what you have to understand. Most people would have done what you did, including me," she said.

"Would have killed?"

She nodded. "If all *that* had occurred."

In our final session she recommended that I go back to Boca de Cangrejo, try to find out what really happened. But I was afraid to go and admitted it.

A month after I graduated, the burning-alive dream returned and I decided the only way to rid myself of the haunting was to take the psychiatrist's recommendation. I didn't tell Samuel J. Toland. He might have volunteered to go, though it might mean reliving the four days of fear. My boyfriend borrowed a Jeep, and we set out for Boca de Cangrejo on the wild chance that Raul Clemente was still there.

Despite the fact that seven years had passed, the trail to Boca looked much the same as when my father and I had traveled it so long ago. Even the rock that said Rijo was still there, and we made the same sharp turn westward toward the Cortez.

And when we reached the sea, on a sunny October Saturday, Isla Viernes Dulce also looked the same as the first time I'd seen it—a mound of blue-gray on the horizon, set in golden waters.

But Boca de Cangrejo had changed somewhat.

There were now about twenty-five houses along the beach, spread almost evenly in each direction from the cantina. A dozen fishing skiffs instead of two were pulled up to await high water.

We stopped in front of the cantina, and this time I didn't see eyes peeping at us from doorways and windows.

Children went about their play as if visitors were no longer a novelty; and the gas pump, at last, had been hooked up. Little Boca seemed to be prospering.

From outward appearance, however, the cantina hadn't changed very much, and we went on inside. There, standing behind the counter, was the tall, distinguished figure of immaculate Raul Clemente. Naturally he was older. There was some gray at his temples, but he was as darkly handsome as ever.

I looked over at the hamper of dried fish, half expecting to see the miserable old crone with the drilling eyes, perched again on her barrel. She wasn't there.

I went on up to Raul Clemente and asked, "Do you remember me, Mr. Clemente?"

Scanning me carefully, he replied, "I seem to. There's something I remember about you, I don't know what."

"My father and I came here seven years ago at Easter to camp on Isla Viernes Dulce. . . ."

Clemente stared at me a moment longer, then said, "Ah, yes, I do remember. Yes, I know who you are. You've grown up. You're a lady now. What can I do for you?"

I said, "Tell me who that old man was, and the woman who sat on the barrel over there. We've driven almost three hundred miles to find out."

He smiled. "That's a long way just to ask a question."

"Why did she hate my father? Why did the old man do all those things to us on Sweet Friday? I see him in nightmares."

"They're both dead now. What difference does it make?"

I said, "The nightmares. I see him trembling; I see his mouth in an O; I see him dead. I almost killed him, you remember."

"He was my father," said Clemente, crossing himself.

I'd thought of that possibility.

"And the woman was your mother?"

Clemente nodded, crossing himself again.

"But why was your father out there? I can't think of a worse place to live."

"I can," said Clemente. "There are many worse places. Institutions for the criminally insane, for instance. We did not want him to go there."

"What had he done?"

"Killed a gringo in Sonoyta." Clemente paused thoughtfully. "He did not mean to. His mind had gone bad just before that. But we loved him, my mother and myself, and when the police came looking for him, we hid him on Isla Viernes Dulce and said he'd drowned."

I nodded as the whole four days unfolded again. We'd camped on the wrong island at the worst possible time.

"What was unlucky about your father was that he looked exactly like the gringo my father had killed at Sonoyta. So you see, my father was being visited by that ghost from the moment your boat was beached. Do you understand?"

I said I did. Then I thanked him.

He nodded and asked, "And how is your father?"

I replied, "He doesn't go camping anymore. He hasn't gone camping since that Easter week."

As a matter of fact, that applied to me, too.

We had a soft drink in the pleasant old cantina and then got on the trail back across the desert and up to Mexico 2.

The nightmares ended, but the questions raised by all that happened on Sweet Friday Island linger on. I'll narrow them down to one. Are any of us capable of killing another human being to save a loved one?

I, Margaret Anne Toland, think so.

6/91